SUN–KISSED CHRISTMAS

a SUMMER novel

More Summer Fun!

Beach Blondes

Spring Break

Tan Lines

SUN-KISSED CHRISTMAS

a SUMMER novel

KATHERINE APPLEGATE

Simon Pulse
New York London Toronto Sydney

This book is a work of fiction. Any references to historical events, real people, or real locales are used fictitiously. Other names, characters, places, and incidents are the product of the author's imagination, and any resemblance to actual events or locales or persons, living or dead, is entirely coincidental.

alloyentertainment

Produced by Alloy Entertainment

151 West 26th Street, New York, NY 10001

SIMON PULSE

An imprint of Simon & Schuster Children's Publishing Division

1230 Avenue of the Americas, New York, NY 10020

First Simon Pulse paperback edition October 2010

Copyright © 1996 by Daniel Weiss Associates, Inc and Katherine Applegate

Originally published by An Archway Paperback

For information about special discounts for bulk purchases, please contact Simon & Schuster Special Sales at 1-866-506-1949 or business@ simonandschuster.com.

The Simon & Schuster Speakers Bureau can bring authors to your live event. For more information or to book an event contact the Simon & Schuster Speakers Bureau at 1-866-248-3049 or visit our website at www.simonspeakers.com.

Designed by Tom Daly

The text of this book was set in Bembo Standard.

Manufactured in the United States of America

2 4 6 8 10 9 7 5 3 1

Library of Congress Control Number 2010922985

ISBN 978-1-4169-9397-1

ISBN 978-1-4424-0959-0 (eBook)

To Michael

Deck the Halls with Vows of Folly

On December nineteenth, on a sweltering Florida afternoon, Summer Smith decided to boycott Christmas.

If she could have canceled the whole shebang, she would have, but as far as she knew, that was a power reserved for Santa or Congress, or maybe the Toy Manufacturers Association of America. So she simply vowed to cancel her own personal Christmas, to let it pass unremarked, just another day on the December calendar.

For a girl who flossed nightly, wrote polite thank-you notes the day after her birthday, and always used turn signals when changing lanes, this was a radical move.

But as she stood in the Christmas tree lot late that afternoon, Summer knew she'd made the right decision. Sure, all the standard signs of Christmas were in evidence—things that usually filled her with anticipation. The sharp, piney scent of the trees. The string of Christmas lights, blinking erratically like an out-of-practice chorus line. Santa, cheerfully waving to passersby.

Unfortunately, the scent of pine was nearly overpowered by the smell of coconut oil wafting over from the beach. The lights were dangling off palm trees. And Santa was wearing Ray-Bans and a pair of bright red swim trunks.

In Minnesota, where Summer came from, self-respecting Santas did not wear Ray-Bans. In Minnesota, they put lights on evergreens. In Minnesota, the powers that be had the decency to provide a nice, thick blanket of snow. Sometimes several blankets. Mattresses, even.

With a sigh, Summer grabbed a small, spindly tree, shorter than she was, not to mention thinner. When she shook it, brown needles rained down like dandruff. It matched her mood perfectly.

"This is, without a doubt, bar none, the most pathetic excuse for a Christmas tree I have ever seen," Marquez, Summer's best friend, pronounced.

"It is, isn't it," Summer said, looking pleased.

"I was wrong. That's not a tree," Marquez continued.

"That is a twig with delusions of grandeur."

Summer motioned to her cousin, Diana. "I need a second opinion."

Diana rolled her eyes. "You want a second opinion? Call Dr. Kevorkian."

"Fine. Whatever. Forget it." Summer said. "Let's just put some tinsel on that dying philodendron in the kitchen. But the way, I am officially quitting Christmas."

Marquez and Diana exchanged a "yeah, right" look.

"You can't quit Christmas," Diana informed her. "It's just one of those things. Like SATs and periods."

Summer leaned her tree against the fence. "What's the point? Let's face it, this Christmas is going to be a dud for all three of us. Our families are spread all over the place. There's no snow, which, I'm sorry, is so completely *not* merry. We're all broke—" She glanced at her cousin. "Well, two of us are, anyway. All these trees are half dead. Santa's wearing swim trunks and he's got a tattoo on his calf. Did I mention there's not even, like, one flake of snow? And oh, yeah. I'm flunking out of my first semester of college."

Marquez draped her arm around Summer's shoulders. "Summer, you got two A's, a B-plus, and a B. That does not constitute flunking out. If it does, I'd better apply to that Sally Struthers trucking school, because I am in major academic trouble."

"I took an incomplete," Summer reminded her

glumly as they wandered down another row of trees.

"Which you're going to finish up this week," Diana said. She paused to check out a tall pine with long, droopy needles. "You're just going through withdrawal, Summer. You've been on this extended school high all semester, and now that you've finished exams you don't know what to do with yourself."

Summer examined a wreath wrapped with a red bow. She crushed some of the pine needles between her fingers to release the scent. Unfortunately, the needles were made of plastic. She sighed. "Maybe you're right, Diana. It was a pretty great semester overall. Maybe I'm just feeling a little let down."

Let down and a little lost—that was the truth. Now that exams were over, Summer had time to think about things that she'd really rather not think about. Such as the fact that her parents had split up and were spending Christmas apart for the first time in more than twenty years. Such as the fact that Austin Reed had found a new girlfriend.

Marquez pointed out a tree. "How about this one? It's not too shabby."

"Are you sure you want to bother?" Summer asked.

"We have to," Marquez said. "It's part of the magic of the holidays."

"I sort of feel sorry for mine now," Summer said. "It's like we rejected it."

Marquez rolled her eyes at Diana. "Oh, let her get the twig. She's vulnerable," Marquez said. "Summer takes Christmas very seriously."

"Not anymore," Summer argued.

"Are you not the person who suggested—in the middle of exams—that we try making our own candy canes from scratch?" Marquez shook her head so hard her dark curls bounced. "I mean, really. Who knew you could actually *cook* them?"

"Where did you think they came from?"

"I thought they harvested them. Candy cane farms somewhere snowy. Finland or Latvia. Or your native land, Minne-so-dead."

"I was just trying to get you two into the spirit," Summer said. "Which I've now officially given up on."

"Uh-huh. This from the girl who's seen every Christmas movie ever made and forced us to sit through them? *White Christmas. Miracle on 34th Street. It's a Wonderful Life*, like seventeen times in a row."

"Three times," Summer corrected. "It's a holiday classic. Look, let's just grab a tree and go, okay? I need to get some work done on my history project. My overdue, incomplete, probably-will-get-an-F-minus project. Did I mention there's no snow in this town?"

"Summer, you live in the Keys. Much farther south and we'd be in Cuba," Diana said. "Snow is not an option."

They went back to retrieve Summer's tree. It was gone.

Diana laughed. "Someone actually bought the thing?"

"Maybe they're putting it out of its misery," Marquez suggested.

Summer caught sight of her tree being dragged toward the exit and followed it. The tree thief was halfway out the gate by the time she caught up with him. When he turned around, she sucked in her breath.

He was tall with dark hair, the hint of a beard, and a deep tan. And he just so happened to be her ex-boyfriend.

"You stole my tree."

Austin Reed smiled and cocked his head at her. "You picked out this tree?"

She gazed at him, unable to pull her eyes away. She hadn't seen Austin in a long time. His hair was a little shorter and his shoulders—was she imagining this?—a little broader. "I have dibs, Austin," she said in a faint voice. In the background, she could hear Marquez and Diana whispering ferociously behind a wall of wreaths.

He shook his head. "Would you consider joint custody?"

Summer reached for the trunk. Their fingers brushed.

"How've you been?" Austin asked. Very carefully, not too interested. He was smiling that knowing smile that always made her wonder if he could read minds. She realized suddenly how much she'd missed it.

"Okay. You?" She sounded way too uncomfortable. A ten on the dork-o-meter.

"I haven't seen you since . . . when?"

She wondered if he really didn't remember, particularly since she knew exactly how long it had been. Ten and a half weeks, not that she was counting. "Blythe's party, I think."

"That's right. Yeah."

He'd been with a girl that night. She'd had too-red dyed hair, a nose ring. She'd danced with him very brazenly, watch-me dancing, the way Summer would never in a million years have the nerve to dance. She was just a friend, Austin had said.

But Summer knew that wasn't true. She knew because her brother, Diver, shared an apartment with Austin. Given the awkward circumstances, she never visited their place anymore. But she did occasionally request updates from Diver.

"So how's collegiate life?" Austin asked.

"Great, really great. Remember how scared I was? But these last few months, they've been incredible. It's all been so hard and intense, and I still got through it on my own." She paused, trying to prevent herself from sliding into full babble mode. But it was easier to talk than gaze at Austin in silence. "I'm sorry. It's hard to explain."

"You don't have to explain. I know exactly what you mean. I knew you could do it." Austin glanced at their fingers, which were still touching. "How were exams?"

"Tough."

"I'm sure you did great."

"I had to take an incomplete in Intro to U.S. History. We had to do an interview with someone whose life has been affected by a war. My first one fell through, so I got an extension."

"Fell through how?"

"I was going to interview that lady who sells fish by the pier. You know the one I mean? She smokes cigars. Well, she told me she was a volunteer nurse during World War One. But then I did the math and figured she'd have to be, like, a zillion years old."

"You ought to talk to Harris, my dad's uncle. Ask him about World War Two—you can't shut him up."

"How is your dad?" Summer asked gently.

Austin looked away. "He—"

"*There* you are!" A girl, the red-haired nose-ringed girl, sauntered over.

"Esme, you remember Summer?"

"Sure." She flashed Summer a smile. "Hey."

"Hi." Summer let her gaze fall for just a split second to the girl's hand on Austin's waist.

"Pukey tree," Esme said.

"It has character," Austin objected.

"It's hideous, Aus. Let's get something artificial. You know, pink or silver. Something outrageous."

Austin pushed the tree toward Summer. "Guess you win. Give it a good home, okay?"

Summer nodded, wishing she hadn't won. "You can have visitation rights."

"You're in the new place now?"

"Yeah, on Full Moon Beach, in one of those old resort cottages. Last one on the right."

"I'll stop by sometime." He paused, staring at her with questioning eyes as if she were a vague acquaintance. Someone he knew he'd shared some laughs with but couldn't quite place.

"Well," Esme said, clearing her throat, "we're off to buy into the true commercialism that is Christmas."

"Say hello to Diana and Marquez," Austin added. "They're hiding discreetly behind the wreaths."

"I will. Nice seeing you again, Esme."

"Yep. Likewise."

2

Psychology 101

"I know it's snowing in Minne-so-dead right now," Marquez said that afternoon as she applied another layer of Hawaiian Tropic to her arms, "but you've got to admit, Summer, this isn't bad. Our own private balcony. Our own private beach. Our own private sunshine."

"I love the sun," Summer said. She adjusted the seat on her dilapidated chaise longue. "I love eighty-degree days. I just think they should come in July, not December."

Diana and Marquez were sprawled on the faded redwood deck, soaking up the last of the afternoon rays. Fifty yards away, the ocean lapped lazily. A handful of seagulls had congregated a few feet from the deck steps. They'd long since learned the girls were an easy touch.

Diana rolled onto her back, her long dark hair splayed out on her beach towel. Even in an old tank suit, she managed, somehow, to look glamorous. "At least admit the fact that this place is a palace compared to Roach Manor."

Summer smiled. The apartment the girls had shared over the summer had been a little on the seedy side. "It's a minor miracle we found this place," Summer said. "If the roof didn't leak so much, it'd be just about perfect."

The house was tiny, part of an enclave of bungalows at the eastern edge of Coconut Key. It was located right between Florida Coastal University, the college Marquez and Diana attended, and Summer's college, Carlson. The enclave had been a popular resort in the thirties and forties but had long since fallen into disrepair. The owner, a reclusive old guy who'd made a fortune as an art dealer in Miami, refused to sell the property. He rented the houses to artists, students, and other "ne'er-do-wells," as he put it.

Marquez, an art student herself, had gotten his okay to paint a mural on the side of the house. She'd already started a bright, abstract portrait of the three girls, full of sharp edges, out-of-place limbs, and extra eyes.

Marquez, as the artist, had also merited an extra breast.

Summer's brother joined them on the deck. "Your tree's up," Diver announced. "It's kind of spindly, but if you layer on enough decorations, no one will notice."

"That's always been Marquez's philosophy on makeup," Diana said.

Marquez retaliated with a squirt from her water bottle. She missed Diana and hit one of the seagulls instead, causing a mini-riot of flapping wings and outraged cries.

"To tell you the truth," Summer said when the gulls had calmed down, "I'm not really in the mood to decorate."

"You'd better get in the mood," Diana chided. "This is your last chance. Don't forget Marquez and I are playing reindeer at the children's charity thing tomorrow. Right, Blitzen?"

Marquez shook her head. "Don't remind me. I suppose you get to be Rudolph?"

"I helped organize the party. That makes me the senior reindeer."

Marquez nudged Summer with her foot. "How'd you luck out of skipping this party, anyway?"

"I'd love to go," Summer said. "But I've got to do my stupid history thing."

"Well, I'm just saying it's going to be hard to get

motivated," Marquez said. "Summer has a point about Christmas. To me, Christmas means family. And my whole family's in Texas. They can't afford to come here, and I can't afford to go there."

"You think that's bad?" Diana said. "My mom's on another book tour." Diana's mother was a well-known romance author. "She could have flown home, I guess, but I think she's really chasing after some guy she met in L.A. who claims he's a count. Surname Dracula, I'm sure."

Summer glanced at Diver and sighed. This would be their first Christmas since their parents' divorce. Their mom was going to spend Christmas in North Dakota, tending to a sick aunt. Their dad was going to be in New York on business. Both of them were coming down to Florida after the holidays—taking care to ensure that their visits didn't overlap.

"No wonder we're not in the spirit," Summer said. "Our parents aren't exactly setting good examples. Well, Marquez's are, but they're too far away."

"My mom makes these fantastic sugar cookies every Christmas," Marquez said wistfully. "Then my brother Luis tries to scarf them all, and I have to slap him silly and chase him around the house . . . boy, I'm going to miss all those holiday traditions."

"We'll start our own traditions," Diver said, leaning down to kiss Marquez.

Marquez smiled. "You're right," she said. "It'll be fine as long as we're together." She kissed him again. "*If* we're together that is. I feel like I never see you, we're both working so much."

"Are you working the dinner shift tonight?" he asked.

Marquez groaned. "Don't remind me. It's going to be dead. Zero tips." She passed him her suntan oil. "Do my back, would you?"

Summer watched her brother gently apply the oil. He was always so tender with Marquez, so open about his feelings. They made a great couple. It was a reminder of how good a committed relationship could be—and a reminder of how uncommitted Summer was at the moment.

But that, she told herself, was her choice—school first, herself first. Guys later. Much later, when she was emotionally ready. Like, say, when was really, really old. Twenty or something.

Diver looked over at her and smiled. Everyone said they looked alike—same shimmering blond hair, same vivid blue eyes. But there was something centered and calm about Diver that always seemed to elude Summer.

"What're you up to?" he asked, pointing at Summer's notebook.

"My history project. I got an extension till after Christmas, but now I need to find a new subject.

Austin suggested someone, this great-uncle of his, but I don't know. . . ."

"Who else do you have in mind?"

"Well, there's that Vietnam vet, the guy with the beard who runs the Dairy Queen. But he seems a little too enthusiastic about showing me his scars."

"So use Austin's uncle," Diana said, propping herself on her elbows. "What's the big deal?"

Summer noted her cousin's wry grin. Diana *knew* what the big deal was, of course. "It would be a little awkward, is all."

"Awkward because you blew him off?" Diana pressed. "Or awkward because you regret blowing him off?"

Marquez winked at Diana. "She's in denial."

"Yep. She's turned down three perfectly acceptable dates this semester, all because she's pining for the Big A."

"Well, two, anyway. Remember that last one who asked her out, the one who always wore the *X-Files* T-shirt?"

Summer crossed her arms over her chest. "I wasn't pining."

"Come on, Summer," Diana prodded, "you need to accept your feelings."

"I really wish you two hadn't taken that Intro to Psych course," Summer said.

Marquez wagged a finger at her. "And don't forget I have my very own shrink."

"That doesn't qualify you to analyze me."

"No, but it definitely qualifies me to annoy you."

Summer looked up at Marquez and laughed in spite of herself. It was true Marquez had a special talent for annoying her, but Summer was grateful for it. She'd rather have the wild, obnoxious, wise-guy Marquez than the closed, secretive girl Marquez had been last summer. Back then Marquez had been struggling with an eating disorder so severe she'd ended up in the hospital and nearly scared her friends to death. But now with the support of Diver and her friends and her shrink, Marquez was most of the way back to her old hell-raising self.

Summer composed her face as she thumbed through her notebook, smearing suntan oil over her scribbled notes. "I just think if you ask someone to give you some space, that someone deserves the same space himself."

Diana looked at Marquez. "This is all because that someone is dating a *Grind* wanna-be with a nose ring," she said in a loud whisper.

"Diver," Marquez said, "you're Austin's roommate. What's the deal with Esme, anyway?"

"Deal?"

"You know, are they serious or what?"

Diver looked perplexed. "They go out sometimes."

"Duh," Marquez said. "We *know* that. We want to know details."

"Juicy details," Diana concurred.

"No, we don't," Summer said.

"I hardly ever see Austin," Diver said. "We both work so much, it seems like we're never even in the apartment at the same time. And anyway, Esme's his business."

"Guys!" Marquez groaned. "What exactly do you talk about, if you don't talk about relationships?"

Diver grinned. "You know. Guy stuff. Carburetors. Football scores. Burping technique."

"Let me put it this way, Diver," Diana said. "How many toothbrushes are there in your bathroom?"

"Two, I guess." Diver bit his bottom lip, giving it some thought. "Red, blue. Austin's and mine."

"See?" Diana said to Summer. "It can't be that serious. There's hope."

"Diana's right. You've got to go for it, girl." Marquez wiggled her brows suggestively. "It was obvious at the tree lot that he's still in love with you. He was sending you clear signals."

"He was not. He was just being friendly."

Diana shook her head. "Didn't you notice his body language? The tilted head, the flirtatious smile"

"Don't forget the pouting, come-hither lips," Marquez added.

"You'll see when you take psych. It's scientific," Diana said. "Austin was sending you signals."

"Yeah?" Summer said. "Then what exactly did Austin's hand on Esme's butt signal?"

Diana shrugged. "It signals he's conflicted."

"I see."

"And it's your job to unconflict him," Marquez added.

Summer lay back in the chaise longue with a sigh. "Look, it's simple. I told Austin to get on with his life. It's over between us. I had my chance. I wasn't ready when he was ready. And I'm okay with that. Now could you two please try to be okay with it too?"

Diana looked at Marquez. "Her arms are crossed, her hands are clenched."

"And I think her right eye is twitching," Marquez added.

"Which means what, exactly?" Summer demanded.

Marquez patted her on the head, grinning. "Poor thing. And we thought *Austin* was conflicted."

3

The Most Fakest Reindeer of All

"Why couldn't we have been elves?"

Marquez demanded, her voice muffled inside her papier-mâché reindeer head. She adjusted her antlers with an annoyed tug. "The elves get those cute little red cheerleader skirts."

"Quit whining. I'm the one who has to wear the light-up nose, which keeps falling off. It's like having the world's biggest zit. Besides, you're doing a good deed."

"No wonder I'm in such a bad mood."

Diana grinned. Marquez was just being ornery. Even sweating in her faux-fur Rudolph costume, Diana found it easy to get caught up in the spirit of things.

A friend and fellow volunteer at the Dolphin Interactive Therapy Institute, where Diana had been working for over a year, had urged her to help at this Christmas party for low-income families, and Diana was glad she'd agreed to sign up. She surveyed the large, festively decorated hall. Red-and-green crepe paper hung from the ceiling, Christmas carols blared from a pair of speakers in the corner, and along one wall a table sagged under the weight of donated baked goods. Children raced about, propelled by sugar and anticipation. Santa was due to arrive with gifts at any moment.

A chubby little boy in a red bow tie tugged on Diana's mittened hand. "Make your nose light up," he commanded.

Diana yanked obediently on the string hidden inside her right sleeve. Her nose lit up. She bent down to get at eye level.

"Who's the most famous reindeer of all?" she asked, but for the third time that day, her nose popped out, bulb and all, dangling by a black wire.

"Most fakest is more like it," the little boy grumbled.

"Watch it, kid," Marquez warned. "She's tight with Santa."

Diana rushed to a corner to reinsert her nose. "How do those Disney World people do it?" she wondered. "Stuck in those Mickey Mouse costumes in ninety-degree heat . . ."

"For starters, they get paid," Marquez muttered. She jerked her head toward the exit. "I gotta pee and get some air. Want to come?"

"We have to be back in time for presents."

"Come on. Even Rudolph has to relieve himself now and then."

The girls grabbed their purses and headed discreetly down the hall toward the women's rest room. Diana poked her head in the door, then retreated.

"We can't go in there," she reported. "It's full of kids. They see us headless, they'll have nightmares for years."

"Kids are pretty sophisticated, Diana," Marquez replied. "I kind of doubt they're buying you as a reindeer. I mean, you're carrying a purse. How many reindeer haul Tampax and Tic-Tacs around with them?"

After a few minutes of searching, they located another rest room at the end of a row of offices. It featured a small, separate lounge area with a yellow vinyl bench, two chairs, and a well-used ashtray.

A young girl, maybe seventeen, lay on the couch. She was on her side, head propped on a duffel bag, hugging her knees. She opened her eyes and stared at the two costumed intruders without reaction.

"Oh," Diana said, "sorry. We just wanted to take our heads off."

"Be my guest." The girl waved her arm. "I don't exactly own the place."

"I thought maybe you were . . . you know, napping or something."

"Thinking," the girl said flatly. She had white-blond hair, dark at the part, and eyes rimmed with thick eyeliner. Her face was as pale and empty as a blank sheet of paper.

Marquez yanked off her head. Her olive skin had a sheen of sweat, and her curls were even more incorrigible than usual. "This thing's better than a sauna. I'll bet I lose three pounds of water weight."

Diana cast her a watch-it look. Marquez still showed a tendency to obsess over her weight once in a while, and Diana always pounced on it.

"I didn't mean anything by it, Mom," Marquez said. She poked Diana with her antlers.

Diana ripped off her own head. "Prepare to die, you knave!" she cried, making a quick sword thrust with her antlers.

Marquez countered, dancing across the floor. "She thrusts, she parries, she goes in for the kill!" she shouted, aiming her antlers at Diana's throat.

Just then a stall door opened. A little girl came into the lounge. She blinked doubtfully at the dueling half reindeer, her mouth pursed.

Diana yanked on her reindeer head. "Marquez," she hissed, "your head."

"What?"

"Put on your head."

"It's a little late for that, Diana."

"My name is Rudolph," Diana told the little girl. She knelt down. "And what's your name?"

The girl stared at her, unmoved. She had shimmering white-blond chin-length hair, like the girl on the couch. Diana wondered if they were sisters.

"She's okay," the older girl said. "I told her Santa's bogus."

"Bogus!" Diana exclaimed, making a show of lighting her nose. "I happen to know Santa, and—"

"Give it up, Diana," Marquez advised.

Reluctantly Diana removed her head. She smiled lamely at the little girl. "Want to see how I light up his nose?"

The girl watched, huge blue eyes focused in total concentration as Diana demonstrated.

Marquez took a chair. "I'm sure I believed in Santa till I was, like, six or seven. How old is she?" she asked the older girl.

"Four and a half."

"Your sister?"

"You writing a book?" the older girl snapped.

Marquez pointed to the book lying next to the girl's purse on the floor and then nodded at Diana. "Actually, her mom's the book writer."

Diana groaned. The well-thumbed paperback was one of her mom's best-sellers, *Sweet Savage*. The cover featured a breathless maiden and an Indian with pecs so large he could have used an underwire bra.

"No way. That's your *mom?*" the older girl asked, sitting up. "Mallory Olan?"

"That depends. Did you like the book?"

"Yeah, for a bathtub book."

"Meaning?"

"You know." The girl shrugged, showing a glimmer of a smile. "You read it while you're taking a bath, and if you drop it, it ain't the end of the world or nothin'."

"Finally, an astute critic." Diana grinned. "Yeah, she's my mother. I'm Diana Olan."

Marquez smiled. "And I'm Marquez."

"Maria Marquez," Diana added.

"But anyone who calls me Maria risks a painful death."

The girl hesitated. "I'm Jennie."

"So you like her mom's books, huh?" Marquez asked.

"Well, they're, like, totally unbelievable, I know that. But it's a way to escape for a little while. Go on a trip, kind of. Sometimes, you know, you just need some time away." She eyed Diana with a mixture of curiosity and wariness. "You must be really rich."

"Stinking," Marquez said.

Diana shifted uncomfortably. Marquez, whose dad had lost his job a while back, enjoyed harassing her about her money. Diana tried to be generous, tried not to make a big issue out of it, but it was always lurking beneath the surface of their friendship.

The little girl tugged on Jennie's sleeve. "Can we go to the party, Mom?"

Diana shared a look with Marquez. Like Diana, she was doing the math. Maybe Jennie was older than she looked, twenty, twenty-one. Still, it was hard to believe this was actually her kid.

"In a minute," Jennie said, gently combing the little girl's hair with her fingers. "Here." She pulled a dirty stuffed lamb out of her duffle bag. "Play with your lamb for a minute."

"There's lots of good food at the party," Marquez said. "Punch, Christmas cookies. You should definitely check it out."

The little girl looked at her gravely. "Last year we forgetted to have Christmas."

"Quiet, Sarah." Jennie shrugged. "The truth is, we're sort of crashing this party. A friend of mine on food stamps told me about it. You're supposed to sign the kids up at social services, but it slipped my mind. . . ." Her voice trailed off. "So, anyway, you live around here?"

Diana nodded. "On Coconut Key."

"You must live in, like, a mansion or something."

"No, just a little rental place."

"But your mom—"

"Well, yeah, she has a house on Crab Claw Key."

"It looks like Barbie's Dream House," Marquez volunteered.

"Lots of bedrooms," Jennie said quietly. It was not exactly a question.

"The party, Mom," Sarah said softly.

"In a minute." Jennie smiled at Diana. "So where exactly do you two live?"

"Those bungalows at the end of the key near FCU," Diana said. "You know the ones on Full Moon Beach? Nothing fancy. But a nice view." Diana looked at Marquez and cleared her throat. "Well, we should get going, Blitzen."

"I gotta pee first," Marquez said. "It's going to take me an hour to get out of this costume."

Diana left the lounge and went to the sink to brush her hair. She couldn't see Jennie and Sarah, but she could hear Jennie talking softly to the little girl.

With a sigh, Diana splashed some water on her face. These costumes were way, way too hot for Florida. She wondered if they could be dry-cleaned. She wondered if they'd *ever* been dry-cleaned.

When she returned to the lounge, Sarah was sitting on the couch. Jennie was gone.

"Where's your mom?"

Sarah shrugged. "Coming back."

"Oh. That's good. That way you'll be just in time for Santa Claus."

The little girl nodded solemnly.

A few moments later Marquez joined them. "Where's Jennie?"

"I don't know. The little girl said she was coming right back."

Marquez started for the door, but Diana hesitated. "Maybe we should wait till she gets back," she whispered.

"We'll miss the big Santa entrance. Aren't you supposed to be there, Rudolph-with-your-nose-so-bright?"

Diana glanced at the floor. Jennie's book was gone—her purse and duffel bag too.

She smiled nervously at Sarah. "You wait here, Sarah. We'll be right back," she said.

Diana grabbed Marquez's arm and slipped out the door. "I have a bad feeling about this," she said. "Do me a favor. Check the hall for Jennie. And maybe the parking lot too."

"You think she just . . . *left* her here?"

"Her purse is gone."

"Oh, man." Marquez started down the hall. "Wait here."

Diana returned to Sarah. The little girl was talking to her stuffed lamb. There was something tucked under the frayed ribbon around the lamb's neck. A folded square of paper.

"What's that, Sarah?"

"My mom put it there."

"Could I look at it?"

Sarah handed her the little worn lamb. The folded paper was a page torn out of Jennie's book.

Around the margins was a hastily scribbled message: *Please take care of Sarah till I get back. I promise I just need a little time. Merry Christmas.*

⸎

Summer was lying on the redwood deck, her head resting on her U.S. history book, when the phone rang in the living room. Her sun-stun was so severe it took her a moment to find her way to her feet. She pulled open the sliding glass doors and caught the phone on the fourth ring. "Hello?"

"Get the tree home safe and sound?"

Summer felt her breath catch. She hadn't heard Austin's voice over the phone in a long time. "Yes," Summer said, trying to even out her breathing. She surveyed the overdecorated, feeble-looking stick in the corner. "In fact, it's wearing a string of lights, some tinsel, and a few candy canes. It looks regal. Sort of."

She tried to ignore the long silence that followed. Austin had called her, after all. It wasn't her duty to make it less awkward. Besides, she couldn't think of anything to say.

"Look, I was thinking about that project of yours," Austin said. "The history thing? I really think my great-uncle Harris might be just what you're looking for. Get him started on war stories and he can go on for days. That's what you need, right? Like an oral-history kind of thing?"

"Yeah," Summer said cautiously. "But I think I've sort of got somebody lined up."

"Oh."

"That Vietnam vet at the Dairy Queen. He was supposed to call me this morning to set something up."

"I don't know, Summer. Every time I go in there, he tries to show me his scars."

"Yeah, he tried that on me too. I guess that could be a drawback."

"Harris lives in Cape Heron. It's about an hour's drive from here. I could give you his number."

"Okay. Just in case the Dairy Queen guy turns out to be too weird."

Austin paused. Summer heard him whispering something, then the sound of a girl's muffled voice.

"Listen, the thing is, I've been meaning to see

Harris, anyway. So I could give you a lift over. You know, if you wanted."

Summer cleared her throat. "Don't you think it could be . . . kind of awkward?"

"Awkward why?"

"You know. Esme."

"Oh, she's fine with it."

Summer hesitated. "You're sure?"

"Absolutely."

Okay, then," Summer agreed. "When's good for you?"

"I've got the afternoon off. Let me give Harris a call and see how things look, then I'll firm up the time with you." He paused. "It'll be fun. Harris is a great guy. And you and I can talk over old times."

"Thanks, Austin."

"No problem."

Summer hung up the phone. Her pulse hummed in her throat. Her palms were damp.

No problem at all.

4

Santa's Little Helpers

Diana sat next to Sarah on the couch. Sarah looked at her with wide, questioning eyes. She had impossibly long lashes. Her T-shirt was too big for her tiny frame. The laces of her dusty tennis shoes were untied.

"Want me to tie those?"

She gave a small nod, watching intently as Diana tied each shoe. "Do you know where your mommy went, Sarah?" Diana asked casually.

The little girl shook her head.

"What did she say when she left?"

Sarah studied the loops in her laces. "She loves me."

"That's all she said?"

Sarah gazed pensively at the door. Suddenly it

popped open, revealing a breathless Marquez, her reindeer head tucked under her arm.

"Hey, Rudy. Come here, quick."

"Be right back, Sarah."

Diana slipped out into the hallway. "Well?"

"I can't find Jennie anywhere. But one of the elves saw a blond girl hightailing it out of the parking lot in a blue Chevy just now. Also, Santa's really p.o.'ed that his senior reindeer is missing in action. I told him you flushed your nose down the toilet by accident."

Diana groaned. "This is not good. This is definitely not good. She left a note."

"What did it say?"

"Let me put it this way. Do you prefer to be called Mommy or Mom?"

"Oh, *man*." Marquez let out her breath. "So what do we do? Call somebody, like social services or something?" she demanded.

"How should I know what we do? I don't have a clue."

Marquez leaned against the wall. Children's laughter floated on the air, followed by a loud "ho-ho-ho." "Where's the real Santa when you need him?"

Diana toyed with her Rudolph nose. "How old do you think Jennie was, anyway?"

"I don't know. Twenty-one?"

"No wedding ring."

"And she's obviously broke."

"How can you be so sure?" Diana asked.

"Well, first off, she's here for this party. And second, she was way interested in your mom and the house and all." Marquez shook her head. "Look, I think we should call someone. Or maybe one of the organizers here would know what to do."

"They'll put her in a foster home."

"Probably."

"At Christmas," Diana said. "A foster home with strangers."

"Could be it'd be better for her."

Diana opened the door a crack. Sarah had untied her shoes and was attempting to retie them.

"Jennie looked so tired," Diana said, closing the door. "Maybe she just needed a break. Maybe she was just so worn out—"

"So she decided to take a little nap while peeling out of the parking lot doing eighty?"

"Her note said she was coming back, Marquez. It said she just needed a little time."

"My mom had six kids and no money. She came here from Cuba with nothing. She got way tired. And she never pulled a stunt like this."

"But she had your dad."

"Still. That's no excuse."

"Maybe Jennie had something to do," Diana

ventured. "Fill a prescription. Buy animal crackers. I
don't know, some motherly thing a mother would do."

"Mothers don't just run out on their kids, Diana."

Diana shrugged. "Mallory used to. Whenever the
spirit moved her."

"But your mom left you with a baby-sitter."

"An au pair."

"So a baby-sitter with an attitude. The point is, she
never left you in a bathroom with a couple of moldy
reindeer."

"I remember one time she met this guy, three days
before Christmas . . ." Diana hesitated. "Never mind.
Long story."

She opened the bathroom door again. Sarah looked
at her expectantly. Her dirty T-shirt was ripped at one
shoulder. Her face was smudged.

Diana let the door slowly close. She felt herself
coming to a decision—the kind of decision she'd kick
herself for later. The kind of decision that would give
Marquez ammunition for years of I-told-you-so's and
sarcastic comments.

"Diana?" Marquez nudged her arm. "Listen to me.
We can't take care of her. Remember when Summer
wanted to adopt that stray kitten and we had a big roomie
meeting and decided we weren't mature enough to handle the responsibility of changing a litter box every day?"

Diana nodded vaguely.

"Diana. We are immature. All the forks we own are from Taco Bell. Summer sleeps with that stuffed animal, that weasel football mascot."

"It's a gopher."

"I snort milk through my nose almost every day. And last Saturday I caught you watching *Dora the Explorer*." Marquez tugged frantically on Diana's fur-covered arm. "We are not—I repeat, *not*—mature. That kid in there is probably more emotionally mature than we are."

"Still . . ."

"Think back, Diana. Think back on all those awful babysitting low points. The tantrums, the pouting, the—" Marquez narrowed her eyes. "Wait a minute. You've never babysat in your life, have you?"

"Not exactly. Although a friend of my mom's brought her daughter to dinner once, and I helped her color in her coloring book. It was fun."

"Fun? *Fun*? Let me tell you about fun, Diana. It is not fun calling nine-one-one when the kid you're babysitting gets her arm stuck in the toilet because she thought she saw an alligator. It is not fun trying to unglue a kid's tongue from the freezer. It is not fun removing a sour ball from some unfortunate child's nostril."

"Boy, you sat for a rough crowd."

Marquez paused briefly, her cheeks reddening.

"Um, actually, I think I did all those things. I was kind of a hyper kid. The point is, taking care of a kid is a twenty-four-hour-a-day job. You are, forgive me, a spoiled rich kid. You've never even had a four-hour-a-day job."

"I volunteer at the Dolphin Interactive Therapy Institute."

"I know. And you're great with those kids. But you get to leave them after a couple of hours. You couldn't leave Sarah." Marquez lowered her voice. "Look, I don't want to call social services any more than you do. It sucks. But I don't see any other choice."

Diana chewed silently on a thumbnail.

"Besides," Marquez added, "even if we did keep her, which we can't, how would we ever find Jennie?"

"She knows where we live, more or less. She asked because she's planning on coming back. She left a *note,* Marquez. She said 'till I get back.'"

"So what if she comes back and accuses you of kidnapping?" Marquez demanded. "Maybe she's just after your mom's money."

"I have the note as proof."

Marquez rolled her eyes.

"It's Christmas, Marquez."

"I'd expect that argument from Summer. But you?"

"Just because I didn't want to drape the house in tinsel doesn't mean I don't have Christmas spirit. It's

just . . . subdued. Like in high school, where I sort
of vaguely wanted our team to win, but I still cut out
on the pep rallies." Diana took a deep breath, waiting
patiently. She knew Marquez was coming around. It
was just a matter of time.

"I definitely get to say 'I told you so,' right?"

"You've never asked my permission before."

"But this is big. This is the I-told-you-so to end all
I-told-you-so's," Marquez muttered. "This is majorly
stupid. This is stupid cubed."

"I know. You going to help me or not?"

Marquez peeked inside the bathroom and smiled at
Sarah. She sighed heavily as she let the door close. "I'm
going to regret this."

"Thanks, Marquez."

Diana went back inside. Sarah was talking to her
lamb.

"Hey," Diana said, kneeling down. "Here's the
deal. You mom had to . . . to run an errand. And she
asked me if I would keep an eye on you till she gets
back. Would that be okay with you?"

Sarah considered. "What's an errand?"

"An important thing you have to do."

This required some time to digest. Sarah stared at
her lamb as if they were having some kind of private,
telepathic consultation.

"You know, there was this one Christmas I remember

where my mom had to run an errand," Diana said. "I missed her a lot. But I had a nice time with my au pair."

"A pear?"

"An au pair. She's the person who hangs out with you while your mom runs her errands."

"Did she give you presents?"

"Gretchen? Oh, sure. Lots." Carefully wrapped by a gift-wrapping service. Carefully selected by a gift-buying service.

Diana remembered the doll she'd wanted that year, Li'l Baby Angel. The doll came with wings, a halo, and a hair extension that went all the way to her li'l baby feet. Very much in demand. Parents were starting small riots trying to get their hands on her. Diana had had a name all picked out for her: Veronica, a character in one of her mother's books. She'd told her mother about it a hundred times.

The personal shopper had come through for Mallory. Diana always got everything on her wish list. The card—in block print, not her mother's illegible scrawl—had read, *Here she is, honey! Your new baby, Tabitha.*

Diana had carried the rechristened doll around with her for a year. Tabitha had lost her wings to a teething beagle. She'd lost her wiry hair to Diana's enthusiastic combing and washing efforts. And finally, one day at the mall, Tabitha had been lost altogether.

But Diana still had that card.

"Come on," Diana said. She held out her hand. The sight of Sarah's tiny hand in hers was startling. "I think maybe we're too late for Santa. Sorry. Maybe we can catch up with him later."

Sarah just shrugged. "He forgetted to come last Christmas," she reported again. "So I know he's not real."

"I know how that goes," Diana said softly. "Sometimes the old guy has a lot on his mind."

5

Ex-boyfriends of Christmas Past and Christmas Present

On the way home Diana ran into the Quickie Mart. She bought peanut butter, jelly, animal crackers, milk, and red licorice, all her favorite childhood foods. She also bought a bottle of Bain de Soleil, some Blistex, and a copy of *Sassy*.

Summer was waiting on the porch when they reached the house. She looked way too nice for hanging out—short blue sundress, new hoop earrings, black T-strap sandals she'd borrowed from Diana. She was holding a notebook.

Summer walked down the front steps to greet them. "Who's this?" Summer asked, glancing at Sarah.

"This is Sarah," Diana announced. "She's going to be hanging out with us for a little while."

"Hi, Sarah," Summer said, squatting to give her a smile. "Today, you mean?" she asked, casting a questioning glace at Marquez.

"That's sort of open to interpretation," Marquez said as she unloaded the reindeer costumes from the trunk.

"You can explain that in a minute," Summer said, frowning. "First, guess who called for you, Diana."

"Diana motioned for Sarah to join her on the chaise longue. "It wasn't some girl named Jennie, was it?"

"Some guy. By the name of Seth. Seems he's flying in to visit his grandfather. This afternoon."

Marquez cocked her head at Diana. "Did you already know about this?"

"Well, kind of. I mean, he sort of mentioned it in his last letter, but it was, like, a maybe deal."

"Now it's, like, a real deal," Summer said. "You could have given us some advance warning."

"It's not exactly front-page news," Diana said.

Summer's eyes locked on Diana's, cold and intense. It was rare to get a look like that from sweet, easygoing Summer.

Summer and Diana almost never discussed the big mess between them. Instead they chose to tiptoe around it as though it were a big, ugly piece of furniture in the middle of the living room. Unfortunately, it was almost impossible for Diana not to smack her shin against it once in a while.

Seth was Summer's old boyfriend. More than that, he was her ex-fiancé. But the previous Christmas, when Diana and Marquez had traveled to Bloomington, Minnesota, to visit Summer and Diver and Seth, something had happened. On New Year's Eve, Diana and Seth had been driving home from a party together and gotten trapped in a deep snowbank. One thing had led to another and . . . well, Diana would never again think of Seth as just a friend.

Summer had found out about it six months later. It had effectively put an end to her and Seth's struggling relationship.

It was exactly what Diana had wanted. And one of the few times in her entire life when Diana was ashamed to have gotten her way.

Marquez stepped between them, casting a worried look at Summer. "Hey, I for one like to be updated, Diana. It takes a scorecard to keep track of you three."

Summer shrugged. "It's okay, Marquez. I mean, I've known Seth and Diana were writing each other all fall. It's no biggie. She's been really up front about it." She gave Diana a tolerant smile. "For a change, I've even talked to him a couple of times on the phone when he called for Diana. It's just . . ." Her voice trailed off. "Well, it's weird to think about seeing him."

"I have to pee," Sarah announced.

"Come on," Marquez said. "I'll show you where the bathroom is. We'll let Aunt Diana and Aunt Summer have a discussion without us."

"What's a dishcussion?"

"Louder than talking but quieter than yelling." Marquez held up the costumes. "What do I do with these?"

"I thought we'd have them dry-cleaned," Diana said. "They're not in any hurry to get them back. And it's the least we can do, since we sort of blew our big appearance."

She watched Marquez and Sarah head inside. "So," she said lightly, "you look nice. How come you're all dressed up?"

"I'm going with Austin to meet his great-uncle Harris. And I'm not dressed up." She smoothed her dress. "Am I? Am I, like, way-over-the-top-desperate dressed up? Or just showing-respect-to-your-relative-for-our-interview dressed up?"

"Don't worry. You look just right. Besides, guys never catch the subtleties. All they ever notice is whether you smell good."

"So who exactly is Sarah?" Summer asked, lowering her voice. "And why exactly is she here?"

Diana cleared her throat. "It's a funny story, really. I mean, you're going to laugh when I tell you."

"Why is it I almost never end up laughing when someone says that?"

"See, she was sort of abandoned at the Christmas party. In the bathroom. Her mom—she's, like, *our* age, Summer!—was reading one of Mallory's books. The one with the Indian with cleavage—you know which one I mean?"

"Diana, Austin's coming. I can hear his car. Give me the condensed version."

Diana swallowed. She wasn't used to sounding like a ditz, even a well-meaning one. She was the cool, rational ice queen. In this household, Summer and Marquez were the ones who came up with harebrained schemes.

"We're keeping her."

Austin pulled up in his recently purchased, very old, shuddering green Dodge. Summer kept her eyes glued on Diana. "Keeping her?" she repeated.

"Just until her mom comes back."

"Which will be when, exactly?"

Austin honked. Summer turned to wave. Esme was in the front seat, nuzzling his neck.

"Oh, fantastic," Summer muttered. "This day is getting weirder by the minute."

"I know this stuff with Sarah seems crazy . . . ," Diana said.

"Actually, I think it's really sweet. In a demented sort of way. But even if we all pitch in, Diana, we aren't exactly ready to be parents of the year. The last time you had a pet, you killed it."

"Sarah is not a turtle, and I promise I will not feed her Count Chocula till she explodes."

"What if her mom doesn't come back?" Summer asked gently.

"We'll deal with that if it happens. Which it won't. I hope." Diana sighed. "It's Christmas, Summer. We can't let her be all alone on Christmas."

Diana could tell from Summer's hesitation that she was buying into the idea. Her cousin was an easy touch when it came to Hallmark moments.

"You're right," Summer finally agreed. "That would be awful. Okay, but just till Christmas, though. You really think her mother'll come back?"

"I'm positive."

"I can't be much help because I've got to finish this paper. You think you can handle things?"

"Oh, yeah. No sweat."

Summer gave a dubious smile. "I hope you're right." She put on her sunglasses and turned to go, then paused. "Listen, don't forget to give Seth a call. He said maybe you guys could meet up at the boat parade tonight."

"Are we going to be okay with this? You and me and Seth?"

"And the ghost of Christmas past," Summer added.

Diana looked away. "Let's not talk about Christmases past, okay?" she said softly.

Summer nodded. "I think things will go okay, Diana. If we all just lighten up about everything. Although to tell you the truth, I've never had to hang out with my ex-boyfriend before while he dated someone else."

"Looks like you're about to," Diana said, jerking her thumb toward Austin's car.

"Thanks for reminding me."

"You'll be fine."

The front door opened. Sarah stood there, lamb in tow, waiting for Diana.

"I wish I could say the same for you," Summer said with a smile.

Summer climbed into the backseat. Esme's arm was draped around Austin's neck.

"Hi," Summer said.

"Hi," Austin said.

"Hey," Esme said. She planted a kiss on Austin's neck, leaving a lipstick shadow.

"You smell good," Austin said.

"Thanks," Summer said. Unfortunately, she said it at the same time Esme did.

Well, duh, Summer chided herself. He wasn't talking to you. You could smell like fresh dog poop on the bottom of a sandal and it wouldn't matter to Austin. Unless you got it on his carpeting.

"Es can't come with us," Austin said, looking into the rearview mirror. "We're dropping her off."

"Work," Esme explained.

"Oh. That's too bad," Summer said, sounding not even remotely sincere to her own ears.

Austin pulled out of the drive and hooked up his iPod. It emitted a sinewy, howling sort of sound underscored by loud thumps. Summer wondered what was wrong with the speakers.

"You like Popping Zits?" Esme inquired.

Summer's hand flew to her chin. Why hadn't she used more Clearasil?

"The music," Esme clarified.

"Oh." Summer felt her cheeks heat, no doubt further highlighting her less-than-perfect complexion. "I've never heard of them."

"They're big in clubs around here."

Summer nodded sagely. "The name rings a bell. I haven't been doing a lot of, you know, nightlife. School's totally dominated my life this semester."

"Tell me about it. I thought undergrad life was bad, but grad school's really a killer."

"You're in grad school?"

"Biochem."

Austin nudged her. "For now, at least."

"Austin thinks I should chuck it all and turn to a life of poetry."

"She's a brilliant writer," Austin said.

Summer stared out the open window. Austin had never called *her* brilliant. Come to think of it, no one had ever called her brilliant.

"How old are you, Esme?" Summer asked, holding her windblown hair back with one hand.

"Twenty."

"And you're in *grad* school?"

She shrugged. "I skipped some grades."

"Oh," Summer said. Was that hissing noise coming from the speakers, or was that just the sound of her ego slowly deflating?

Austin drove onto the FCU campus, the college Marquez and Diana attended, and parked next to a small red brick building.

Esme turned to smile at Summer. "Well, duty calls." She pulled Austin to her, fingers twined in his hair, and kissed him. Not a quick good-bye-and-see-you-soon kiss. This was on par with any backseat all-out makeout kiss Summer had ever engaged in. It went on and on and way too on.

Summer opened her notebook, eyes averted. Where was a barf bag when you needed one? She hadn't felt this awkward since Marcie Barrett's eleventh-grade makeout party in her pine-paneled rec room, when Summer had been paired with George "the Droolmeister" Gurtz.

She stared at a blank page in her notebook until she heard the door open. Austin and Esme were just starting to disentangle. Austin's cheeks were flushed.

Summer made a point of staring at her fingernails, convincing herself that she didn't care about Austin's being with another girl. That was fine, that was the deal. But she didn't have to have a front-row seat to one of their tongue-diving exhibitions, did she?

Esme grabbed her purse and climbed out of the car. "Call me," she said. She mouthed the words "Love you."

Austin turned to the backseat. His eyes were a little glazed. He had a smear of red lipstick on the corner of his mouth. Summer decided not to tell him.

He smiled sheepishly.

She took a deep breath. "I'd give it a nine-point-five," she commented coolly.

"What?"

"The kiss. Average technique, but you get points for the high degree of difficulty. What with having an audience and all." She was pleased with the casual tone of her voice.

"Come on up," he said. "You're not going to sit back there the whole trip, are you?"

"I'm allowed in the makeout seat? Would you mind wiping up the saliva first?"

Austin rolled his eyes. "Sorry. Esme is a little, um, demonstrative."

Summer moved to the front seat. "What's Esme's job?" she asked.

"She's a research assistant. Helping this Ph.D.— something about developing proteins that will keep cancer cells from growing."

Of course. "Back when I worked at the Crab 'n' Conch, I developed a way to pass out lobster bibs and refill iced teas at the same time."

Austin looked over at her. His eyes seemed to clear. He grinned. "I've missed you, Summer," he said softly.

A shrill whistle pierced the air. Esme poked her head out of the second-floor window. "Have fun!" she called.

Austin honked.

Summer gave a vague wave. She'd always wanted to whistle like that, two fingers in her mouth, shrill, attention-getting noise.

"She's something," Austin said under his breath as he backed up the car.

Summer nodded, picking too hard at a hangnail on her thumb. "She's something, all right."

6

Survival of the Fittest

Austin lay in a hammock, eyes closed, on the wide
back porch of his great-uncle's town house. Summer's
laughter floated through the screen door. She and Harris
really seemed to have hit it off. She'd been interviewing him for almost two straight hours.

It occurred to Austin that this was the first real time
he'd spent with her since August. He'd run into her
once or twice since then. They'd talked for a few minutes at Blythe's party, but he'd been there with Esme.

Not that this was a date, really. Austin knew nothing would come of it. Didn't want anything to come
of it They'd broken up, and that was that.

Broken up. He hated that phrase. It conjured up

images of dishes thrown in fury, feelings in a jumble of puzzle pieces that could never be reassembled.

And it hadn't been like that at all. He'd been so cool that day she'd ended it.

She needed time to figure out who she was, she'd said. To be Summer alone, not Summer part of a couple, part of Austin-and-Summer. She needed to concentrate all her energy on college.

No problem, he'd said. He'd said, "I love you, Summer." He'd made a joke of it: "I know you'll come to your senses eventually." He'd told her he could wait.

Only he hadn't waited. He'd met Esme and tried not to look back.

Because waiting, he knew, would have been like promising Summer that he would be there for her forever. And he didn't have forever anymore.

The screen door opened, and Summer slipped out. She was holding a glass of lemonade. The ice cubes clinked liked tiny bells.

"For you." She handed it to him. Her soft cotton dress brushed his arm.

"Thanks." He took a sip, set the lemonade on the floor, put his arms behind his head. "How's it going?"

"Great. Harris is incredible. I just came out to see if you're okay. I feel like I'm sort of hogging him. But Harris said you wouldn't care because you've heard it all a million times before."

Austin laughed. "I'm kind of enjoying just lying here, thinking profound thoughts."

"Such as?"

"Actually, I was thinking about that day when you told me to get lost."

Summer looked away. "I don't think that's what I said, Austin."

"Okay, that you wanted to fly solo."

"I don't think that's exactly what I said either."

"Words to that effect, then."

Silence fell. Austin rocked the hammock, one leg on the floor. Summer moved to the edge of the porch, leaving a touch of her perfume in her wake. She'd worn that perfume all summer. It made him think of vanilla, of sunshine, of kisses under the stars.

"It was a good thing," Austin said. "I think you needed to be on your own. You've changed."

She turned. "I have?"

"You're calmer. More self-confident or something."

She smiled. "Or something."

She always smiled with her whole face—her eyes, her lips. It was the first thing he'd noticed about her. It was, come to think of it, probably the first think he'd loved about her.

"Well, I should get back. Harris said he's got a photo album I can look at."

"Thanks for the lemonade."

Summer opened the screen door, then hesitated. "You know, I think what I said that day was that I needed to be by myself for a while. To figure out who I was and stuff." She shrugged. "Just for the record."

"I stand corrected."

He watched her go, slipping away into the shadows. He'd tried so hard to hold on to her the past summer. She'd been trying to mend her relationship with Seth, the rightful heir. Seth was her first real boyfriend, and later her fiancé, and she had tried to work things out with him until even loyal, steadfast Summer could see it was time to call it quits.

And through it all, Austin had waited. He'd known she was in love with him. He'd known that if he just trusted in fate, she'd see they belonged together.

Fate, it had turned out, had an extremely warped sense of humor.

Still, maybe it was all for the best, his losing Summer. There were a lot of good reasons for them not to be together, actually. Reasons he never wanted to have to tell her.

And he had Esme now. Free-spirited Esme, who never needed to talk about the future. Esme, who read the *New York Times* every day and liked to swim in the nude and claimed to understand the poems he wrote.

All of which, it seemed, were about breaking up with complicated girls with amazing smiles.

Girls who wanted to fly solo.

"So, my lad," Harris said as he and Austin walked the neighborhood later that day, "can I safely assume you're aware that you are sporting a spot of lipstick on the corner of your mouth?"

Austin groaned. He wiped his mouth with the back of his hand. "Man, Summer could have said something."

Harris stopped to observe a mockingbird in a nearby oak. Austin was used to such pauses and detours. His great-uncle couldn't walk ten feet without stopping to examine a plant or watch a bird.

"I suppose I can also safely assume that said lipstick did not belong to the lovely young lady with whom I've been having such an interesting discussion today?"

Austin shook his head. Harris had a way of asking the bluntest questions while sounding as discreet as a British butler. It was a good thing Summer was safely out of earshot back at the house, putting her notes together.

Austin wondered if Harris had already asked her the same question. Probably. He wondered what her replay had been. Something sarcastic about Esme, maybe even with a hint of jealousy?

"Summer and I are just friends, Harris."

"Shame, really. Such a charming girl."

"Things didn't . . . work out."

Harris pointed to a spiny little plant clinging to the oak. "Bromeliads," he said. "Such an evolutionary marvel, getting sustenance from air. Ingenious little plants. Survivors."

He adjusted his straw hat and resumed his stride. Austin had to work to catch up. They were both tall, but Harris had a crisp, efficient way of moving— when he wasn't dawdling over plants—that left Austin breathless. Amazing. The guy was in his seventies.

Harris looked over at Austin speculatively. "And how are you surviving?"

"If I could get sustenance from air too, I'd be all set," Austin said. "Unfortunately, I've had to settle for a job as a waiter."

"School?"

"I'm thinking about going back soon." Austin cringed a little. It was no secret that his great-uncle, who'd spent his whole life teaching botany, was annoyed that Austin had quit college after only one semester.

"That's good. Very good. Your father would have been pleased."

Harris took another sudden detour, this time to retrieve a handful of Spanish moss that had fallen to the ground. He held the tangle of gray-green tendrils in his hand, apparently fascinated.

When he was younger, his great-uncle's absorption with such things had mystified Austin. They were just plants, after all.

But the more he wroteor tried to write—poetry, the more Austin understood Harris's obsession. Austin studied words, plain, everyday words, with the same intensity his great-uncle reserved for leaves and stems and berries.

"Another bromeliad, Spanish moss," Harris said, adjusting his wire-rimmed glasses. "See how thick the skin is? Tough and resilient to reduce water loss." He shook his head. "Wonderful, how adaptable the natural world is. The circumstances can be quite dire, but survival is everything. Air plants adapted to tight living requirements by growing on trees." He looked at Austin. "They didn't fight their circumstances. They adapted to them. And the result, quite surprisingly, is such beauty."

"Why do I feel some kind of plant parable coming on?" Austin asked. He'd meant it as a joke, but it had come out sounding sarcastic and annoyed.

Still holding the Spanish moss, Harris resumed his hearty pace. "I went to see your father a while ago," he said. "It was a couple of weeks before he . . ." He paused, cleared his throat, then continued. "He was . . . not responsive. The Huntington's was so advanced. I'd expected that, of course, but it still came as a shock."

"The last time I went," Austin said flatly, "he didn't know who I was." He said it without emotion, a fact that made him oddly proud. He knew his great-uncle was probably expecting him to break down, but Austin had gotten past all the self-pity and anger. He'd accepted things. It had been his dad's sad genetic fate. And someday it would be Austin's too. A disease that slowly robbed you of your ability to move and communicate. A disease that robbed you of your very soul.

They turned the corner, past too-perfect lawns and more pastel town house clones. Harris had moved to the Keys from New York after his wife of thirty-four years, Louise, had died. To Austin, Harris's move here had never seemed quite right. In the old days, Harris and Louise had owned a big, rambling country home in chronic disrepair with a big, rambling country garden to match. When he was a kid, Austin would visit in the summer and come out of the garden covered with thistles and powdered with pollen from the wildflowers.

By contrast, this place was too sterile. But maybe after losing your wife and retiring from your job, sterile was just what you wanted. Maybe it was easier to be around things that didn't stick to you and stain you.

This time it was Austin who paused. He picked up

a rock, smooth as glass, and rubbed it in his palm. "I have it, Harris," he said softly. "The gene. Dave and I both do."

Harris took the rock from Austin, examined it, then tossed it with a great heave far down the road. "I feared as much," he said. His lower lip trembled, but he tightened it into a firm line. "When I saw your mother at the hospital and asked how you and your brother were faring, there was something about her answer . . . it's hard to put into words. Something in the way she tiptoed around your names, I suppose."

Austin suddenly regretted telling the old man. What was the point? It was cruel, really. Harris would be long gone by the time Austin showed any symptoms of the disease. Up till now, he hadn't told anyone except his mother and brother. Not even Summer, although he'd come close to telling her a thousand times.

"Don't worry, Harris. By the time Dave and I start having problems, they'll have a cure. Look at the amazing stuff they're doing with genetics. They've already found the gene that causes Huntington's. It's just a matter of time."

Harris gave a terse nod. "You're right, of course. That isn't so much what's troubling me. It's the thought of you living your life with that ax hanging over your head. It's the way it may change you."

Austin shrugged. "We all have an ax over our heads

when you get right down to it, right? I mean, face it. Nobody lives forever."

"True enough. And yet I can't help wondering if this is taking its toll."

"Well, sure, I went through my drink-too-much-and-get-all-existential phase. But after a couple of weeks I got tired of dressing in black."

Harris smiled a little. "And your quitting school?"

"That was more about Dad, about not knowing. And about me, I suppose. I was feeling lost. But I'm better now."

"I see. And love?"

"Excuse me?"

"Are you in love? With the red-lipstick girl, perhaps?" Harris paused. "Or perhaps with some other young lady whose acquaintance I've recently made?"

"You know, Harris, I could pry into your love life too."

"That would be a very short conversation indeed," Harris said with a rueful laugh.

They walked in silence for a while. Harris's town house was in sight. The only way Austin could be sure it was his great-uncle's was by checking the name on the mailbox.

Austin slowed his pace a little. "Summer and I . . . things didn't work out, but it wasn't because of my problem. The timing was all off. Just one of those things."

"You didn't tell her?"

"No. I wanted to. I started to a few times. But it didn't seem fair. Actually, I'm sorry I told you."

Harris stopped. He pulled Austin close in an awkward, fierce embrace.

Then, as quickly as he'd reached for him, Harris let Austin go. He walked over to a small elm tree and gently deposited the Spanish moss he'd been carrying onto a branch.

"You'll be fine," he said, turning to Austin. A lone tear rolled down his cheek. "You're a survivor."

7

Love at First Sight and Other Clichés

Summer was deep in thought when she heard voices coming through the yard. A moment later the screen door opened.

"All squared away with your notes?" Harris asked as he and Austin came into the living room.

"Pretty much," she said. "At least I hope so."

With Austin and Harris standing side by side, Summer could see the family resemblance. The wistfulness around the eyes, maybe. Or perhaps it was the secret half smile they both sported, as if only they knew the punch line to some private joke.

"You'll stay for dinner, of course," Harris said, tossing his straw hat onto a carved oak rack.

"Oh, we should be going," Summer said. "I've kept you long enough."

She glanced at Austin, half hoping he'd say "No, let's stay," but he didn't. He probably had plans with Esme for that night. The boat parade, maybe.

"I make the best grilled swordfish in the Keys," Harris said. "With a nice pineapple salsa, maybe some sugar snap peas—"

"Sounds great, Harris," Austin interrupted, "but I've really got to be getting back."

"Date with Esme?" Summer inquired.

Austin shrugged. "Something like that."

Harris cast Summer a discreet smile that seemed to be saying, "Don't feel bad, he'll come to his senses one of these days." Or maybe it was just a discreet smile that said, "I pity you, poor dweeb-girl."

"I do so hate to dine alone. . . ." Harris sighed theatrically.

"What was I thinking?" Austin made a show of checking his watch. "The boat parade doesn't start till nine, and it's only an hour's drive back. Of course we'll stay."

"Shameless manipulation." Harris winked at Summer. "Works every time. So, anything else I can do to help you with your report?"

"I did have a couple of questions about the photo album you showed me."

"Ask away."

"There were some pictures. . . ." Summer flipped through the pages of Harris's dusty album. "Here. Is this the buddy you were telling me about who was killed in France? Mario—" She checked her notes. "Fidanza?"

"Took a bullet in the chest." Harris gazed at the photo. "Cocky-looking kid, hmm? Had this wonderful baritone, used to sing Italian arias to us."

Summer jotted a few words in her notebook. She turned the page. "And here, this woman, the nurse? I was just wondering, since you have a lot of photos of her . . ."

A peculiar look came over Harris. He stared at the photo tenderly. "That would be Vera," he said softly.

Summer exchanged a look with Austin. He shook his head, clearly mystified.

"Was she . . . a friend?" Summer asked.

"Ah, yes. A friend." Harris closed the album. "A man has a friend like that once in his lifetime, if he's been blessed by the stars."

He fell silent. Summer had a feeling he didn't have any more to say. And she didn't want to pry.

But Austin was clearly intrigued. "It seems you've broken new ground, Summer," he said. "This is the first I've heard about Vera." He took the album from Harris and studied the pictures. "Now I'm really intrigued. I've seen this album before, and I don't remember ever seeing these pictures, Harris. And believe me, *her* I'd remember."

"Yes, Vera had a lovely smile," Harris said neutrally. He settled into a leather armchair and began stuffing a pipe with cherry-scented tobacco.

"So what gives with the pictures? How come I've never seen these before?"

"I suppose—" Harris paused to tamp down the tobacco. "—I kept those photos hidden away in the attic in deference to Louise." He smiled at Summer. "My wife of over thirty years."

"But after Louise died," Austin persisted, "you brought these out?"

"An old man, indulging in his memories." Harris gave an embarrassed shrug.

"So indulge us," Austin said with a grin.

"Austin," Summer interjected, "maybe Harris doesn't want—"

Harris waved a hand. "Oh, there's not much to tell, really. It was December 1944, and I took some shrapnel in the leg. Vera was a nurse from California at the Forty-first Evac hospital outside of Maastricht, Holland. It was a huge monastery the Nazis had used for Hitler Youth activities, but the army nurses had turned it into a pretty impressive hospital, given how little they had to work with."

"So you met Vera there and . . . ," Summer

prompted, scribbling away in her notebook.

"And we fell in love instantly." Harris smiled at Summer. "There's a reason 'love at first sight' is a cliché. It's because it really happens. But perhaps you already know that."

Summer felt heat rise up her neck. She carefully avoided looking at Austin. "Um," she said in a flustered voice, "so what happened with Vera? If it's okay to ask?"

"One thing led to another," Harris said. "We had so little time together, but every moment was another miracle. Oh, we had so much we shared, Vera and I! We both loved Bach and chocolate and birding."

"Birding?" Summer repeated.

"Bird-watching. Not that we could see any there, of course. With all the shelling, the birds had all but vanished, it seemed. But listen to me carrying on!" Harris paused and took a deep breath. "The last time I saw her, we had this Christmas dinner planned, the two of us, right before I was due to be sent home. My buddy and I went all over the hospital trying to dig up candles and chocolate and anything else we could get our hands on to make a decent dinner. Ended up with C-rations, mostly, and a lantern for candlelight. Set up a little table in a medications tent. Even recruited some friends to croon for us."

"Very romantic," Summer said, smiling.

"And there was the ring, of course. Used a shoelace for that." Harris shook his head. "What can I say? I was young, foolish, misguided."

"Ring," Austin repeated, "as in engagement?"

"That was the idea, yes. However, the best-laid plans of mice and men . . ." Harris shrugged. "Vera never came that night. I still have that old piece of shoelace. I found out later that she was transferred to another unit. Strange thing was, she requested the transfer. I've often wondered why. . . ."

"Did you ever try to find her?" Austin asked.

"Started to look her up once, after Louise died. Spent all day at the public library going through every phone book in existence. Found her sister Rose in Atlanta. She said Vera was living in Florida. Right here in the same state. Said she'd retired from nursing. Said she'd never married."

"So you called her?" Summer asked.

"No, no. I suppose it was just enough to hear her name again." Harris laughed. "Who knows why we do such things? The heart is an odd muscle indeed."

Summer fumbled in her purse for a Kleenex and blew her nose.

"Now, Summer, it's hardly a cause for tears. I had my Louise, a wonderful woman. A man couldn't have asked for a more devoted companion."

"I'm sorry." Summer sniffled. "It's just that it

sounds like one of those black-and-white war movies on the classics channel."

"It does at that, doesn't it? I do sometimes wish I'd tried harder to find her after the war. . . ." Harris lit his pipe with deliberate care. "But there's no point in second-guessing. Not now."

"Maybe it wasn't meant to be, Harris," Austin said softly.

"I suppose," Harris said. He gazed at Austin with a faraway smile. "I'll tell you this, though. A love remembered with regret is the saddest thing in the world, Austin."

"Maybe so, Harris," Austin replied. "But I'll tell you this. It makes for some great poetry."

Summer watched the string of low-slung buildings along the highway fly by. Tackle shops, surfboard stores, mini-marts, all of them with their garish holiday lights ablaze. She sighed.

"Not quite what you had in mind for Christmas, huh?" Austin said.

"I'm boycotting Christmas. Didn't I tell you?"

"Right. That'll be the day. Trust me, you'll find a way to make Christmas happen."

Austin grinned, and once again Summer was reminded of Harris. Something about that pensive smile. Although to be fair, Harris had a much better haircut.

"Maybe you just have the holiday blues," Austin suggested.

"Who could blame me?" Summer pointed to a flamingo-shaped sign in front of a motel. The bird was outlined in flaming pink neon and sported a tired-looking wreath around his neck. "This is all so . . . so un-Christmassy."

"The boat parade tonight should be nice. All the sailboats, lit up with lights."

"Maybe." Summer stared out the window. "You meeting Esme there?"

"Yep."

Summer tried her best to look indifferent, but a check in the right side-view mirror told her she just looked a little constipated.

"Marquez and Diana are going, I think. Probably Seth too. He's flying in. You could just drop me off there."

Austin looked over at her. "How is my old rival doing?"

"Seth's fine, I guess. We haven't really kept in touch. He and Diana have been calling and writing each other a lot, though."

"And that's . . . okay?"

"Of course it's okay. I'd be thrilled if he found somebody."

"Even if it turns out to be your cousin? Your cousin

who secretly had a tryst with him behind your back? Last Christmas, if I recall the details—"

"I recall the details pretty well myself. And yes, that would be fine with me."

"You're a better man than I," Austin said with a chuckle.

Summer opened her notebook, glancing vaguely at her notes in the fleeting light of the street lamps. The warm, sweet-smelling wind flipped the pages. She *was* okay with Seth seeing Diana. It was weird, sure, and seriously awkward. But she was okay with it. So why wasn't she okay with Austin seeing Esme?

Austin turned right, heading down the long two-lane road that led to the center of town. The sky was a dark violet-blue, fringed with clouds low on the horizon. The ocean moved listlessly, lapping at the pale sand. Through the darkness Summer could barely make out the shape of a small twin-engine plane as it moved beneath the clouds. She watched it slowly bank, lights twinkling like stars.

The first time she'd seen the Keys had been from a plane. She'd been shocked by the dazzling, too-perfect beauty of it, the islands strung out below her like an endless emerald necklace.

The first time she'd set eyes on Austin had been on a plane too.

"There's a reason 'love at first sight' is a cliché,"

Harris had said earlier in the afternoon. "It's because it really happens. But perhaps you already know that."

She remembered it so perfectly. She'd been seat 28-A. He'd been seat 28-B. She'd been munching on peanuts. While he was rifling through his backpack, she'd sneaked a glance at him. He had a couple of tiny silver hoops in his ear and a five o'clock shadow. His dark hair did not seem to be operating under any kind of organizing principle. His denim jacket was ripped and faded.

He'd looked into her eyes, and she'd nearly choked on her peanut. . . .

Summer shook herself from her reverie. "You know what Harris told me he was doing for Christmas? He said he was going to repot a Norfolk pine."

"So?"

"So does that sound like a merry Christmas to you?"

"Depends. You have to understand. For a professor of botany, it's probably the perfect holiday. And back in the old days, when we were kids, Harris and Louise hardly ever came to visit for the holidays. They were always off traveling the world—picking lichens in Ireland or finding medicinal plants in the Amazon."

"He'll be all alone, Austin. Why don't you get together with him? What's your family doing for Christmas, anyway?"

Austin looked uncomfortable. He tapped his fingers

on the steering wheel. "I went home for Thanksgiving," he said slowly. "And my mom, maybe my brother, are coming down here to visit this spring. They're all doing Christmas back home. But I wasn't really up for it." He swallowed. "We were all going to, you know, maybe go visit my dad in the hospital, do up the whole Christmas thing, even though we knew he wouldn't have a clue what was going on. There was this big fight about it. I thought it was a good idea, my brother hated it. My mom . . . well, she wasn't sure. But then my dad kind of went ahead and made the decision for us. He, um . . . my dad died, Summer."

Summer gasped. She touched Austin's shoulder. "Oh, my God. I'm so sorry, Austin. So sorry."

"It's not like it was exactly a surprise. I mean, I think secretly we were all kind of relieved, not that any of us would actually say anything. He was suffering a hell of a lot."

Summer shivered a little, even though the air was warm. "It must have been especially hard for Dave," she said. "Because he knows he has the Huntington's gene, I mean. That's got to be tough."

Austin didn't respond. He slowed to a stop behind a long line of cars heading into a public parking lot near the pier.

"It was hard," he said at last, eyed glued on the truck ahead of them. "Seeing your future mapped out for you is, generally speaking, not a good idea."

Summer studied him cautiously, trying to read his mood. It was almost impossible to talk to him openly about his father. He became so remote, it was hard to express to him how much she cared and how sorry she felt.

"I wish I could have been there for you." Summer hesitated. "I mean, not *for* you. It's not like I could have done any good. But *with* you, you know? I feel like I should have been there. I wish you'd called."

Austin reached over and touched her cheek. "Yeah," he said softly, "I wish I had too."

8

Summer's Bad Idea

I didn't expect there to be so many people," Summer said as she and Austin snaked their way along a dark path toward the beach.

Austin paused, surveying the throng. "Give a yell if you spot Esme."

The marina and the adjacent public beach were brightly lit and filled with people, many of them camped out on blankets or in beach chairs. Vendors in red Santa hats cruised the area, selling everything from red-and-green cotton candy to conch fritters. A high-school marching band was on the longest wharf, playing an off-key reggae rendition of "I'm

Dreaming of a White Christmas." In striped tents on the edge of the beach, sellers hawked their wares.

Summer took in the merchandise as she passed. Handmade ornaments, many featuring flamingos in ski caps. Crocheted Christmas stockings that read Merry Key-Ristmas. Black-velvet paintings of Santa on a surfboard. Suddenly she found herself longing for the nice, wholesome tackiness of the Mall of America, back in Minnesota.

They broke through the crowd and headed to the water's edge, finally locating a patch of sand to call their own. "How about we roost here and hope everybody finds us?" Austin suggested.

Summer nodded, dropping onto the fine white sand. "When do the boats start?" she asked.

"Nine or nine-thirty, I think," Austin said.

A small plane buzzed past, towing a sign that read All U Can Eat Fish at Cap'n Joe's! Xmas Special— 2-for-1 Beer!

Summer smiled. "You know what I was thinking about a while ago?"

"There are no depths to which this country won't sink to make a buck?"

"Well, that too." She picked up a handful of sand and let it drift through her fingers slowly. "I was thinking about that day we met, on the plane."

"You said, 'Hi, I'm twenty-eight-A,' and I was instantly hooked."

"Or was it twenty-eight-B?"

"No, I'm sure it was twenty-eight-A. This is not something I would forget." He leaned back on his elbows and nodded. "As a matter of fact, what you actually said was, "Hi, I'm your seat-meat, uh, mate. Twenty-eight-A.""

"I was stunned into babble by your incredible charm."

"Again, your memory is serving you badly. I was your basic butthead. I didn't want to be on that plane, and I was mad at the entire planet."

Summer nodded. "You were going to see your dad in the hospital. You had every right to be a butthead. And you weren't anyway." She paused. "You were just really sad."

"I can't do this," Austin had said that day, and there'd been such sadness in his dark eyes that for a brief, insane moment, she'd wanted to reach out and hold him.

He'd flipped open his seat belt, grabbed his backpack, and sprinted down the aisle without another word.

She'd noticed his notebook on the floor and picked it up, wondering if she should go after him. Flipping guiltily through its pages, she'd come to an unfinished sonnet that began: *That I have not yet met your gentle gaze* . . .

She remembered feeling a little as though she were rifling through someone's underwear drawer. On the final page was a scrawled note: *Testing Thursday, March 21, 2 p.m., Dr. Mitchell. Outpatient clinic.*

She'd grabbed her purse and run down the aisle, clutching the notebook in her hand.

She'd run off the plane, letting it take off without her, chasing after a complete stranger, even if he did have the most penetrating, sad, tearful eyes she'd ever seen.

It hadn't made any sense.

And it had been the smartest thing she'd ever done. . . .

Austin met her eyes, pulling her back into the present. "Yeah. I was really sad." He reached over and took her hand. "And when I ran off that plane just before it took off, you, for some incredible, unfathomable reason, followed me. Even though you'd been on your way to spend spring break with Seth."

"You left your notebook full of poems. I had to rescue 'Sonnet to a Girl Unmet.'"

Austin let go of her hand. "Never did finish that."

"Maybe," Summer said slowly, "you met the girl." She turned to gaze at the sky. The stars glowed and throbbed in the darkness. "So you didn't need to finish the poem."

For a while Austin didn't respond. At last he shrugged. "Or maybe I met her," he said, "but I was waiting to see how things turned out. Maybe it's time I finished it, after all."

"Entrant number one, *Escape Route*," a loud-speaker blared over the crowded beach.

The crowd broke into applause. Close to shore, bobbing slowly past the marina and beach, was a huge sailboat lit up like a Vegas casino. Every square inch seemed to be covered by blinking Christmas lights. The crew, decked out in elf costumes, danced and mugged for the crowd. Atop the foremast, an illumi-nated mechanical Santa waved jerkily.

"It is kind of pretty," Summer conceded, resting on her elbows in the sand, "in a really tacky way. I suppose I have to give them points for trying. After all, Florida is sort of handicapped when it comes to Christmas weather."

"Snowflake-challenged," Austin agreed.

"Maybe we should have invited Harris along," Summer said.

Austin shook his head. "Harris is like you. He would find this unbelievably tacky. Me, I say nobody does tacky better than Florida."

"You know what just occurred to me?" Summer said. "What would make my paper really interesting?"

"Having turned it in two weeks ago?"

"What would make it interesting," Summer continued, "would be if I looked up Vera to get her take on Harris's story. A sort of double oral history. His and hers."

"Bad idea."

"It's a great idea."

"This isn't a romance you're writing. It's about the effect of war on an individual, isn't it?"

"But war did affect these individuals profoundly," Summer said. "I could find Vera, ask her about things, and—"

"And then reintroduce Vera and Harris," Austin finished. "I know how your mind works, Summer. I don't think it's a good idea."

"Why not?"

Austin paused as the crowd burst into applause for the second entrant, a fishing boat decorated like Santa's sleigh. "Because," he said when the crowd had quieted a bit, "things don't always work out the way we'd like them to. Because you can't write other people's stories for them."

"A Christmas reunion, Austin. Think of it. It would be so romantic! We could even re-create the whole thing, Harris's dinner, the ring . . ."

She could tell by Austin's dubious expression that

he wasn't buying it. "It could make him really happy, Austin," she said. "And if it did work out, it would redeem this whole otherwise crappy Christmas."

"If Vera didn't want to be with Harris fifty-plus years ago, what makes you think anything's changed?"

Summer shrugged. "People change." She looked away. "They make decisions, they change their minds. It happens."

They fell silent, listening to the rise and fall of the noisy crowd, ebbing and flowing like the waves.

"Is that Diana over there?" Austin asked, pointing. "On the wharf, with Marquez and . . ." He frowned. "Is she carrying a little girl?"

"I forgot to tell you. Diana and Marquez are adoptive mommies. Long story." Slowly Summer stood, brushing sand off her legs. "I guess I should get going. Thanks for today."

Austin smiled. A girl's voice called out his name. They turned to see Esme waving as she made her way across the sand.

"Well, good luck with the project, Summer. And if I don't see you, have a great Christmas." Austin leaned toward her and gave her a soft, lingering kiss on the cheek.

Summer's heart ached as she watched him run off toward Esme, darting through the busy crowd. Her throat felt choked, and her vision blurred with tears. She wanted to run after him, to reach out and hold him. To tell him that she loved him and always had.

She couldn't. It wouldn't be fair. It didn't make any sense.

But then, the heart was a strange muscle indeed.

9

The Ghosts of Gifts Past

"There's Summer" Seth said, and Diana felt his hand slip away from her waist.

He waved. Summer waved back as she inched her way through the crowd. As if they were just a couple of old friends, Diana thought. As if they weren't two people who'd planned, once upon a time, to make a life together.

"Marquez, could you take Sarah for a minute?" Diana asked.

"Sure. Hop on board the ol' shoulders, kid," Marquez said. "You'll have the best view in the house."

Her lamb in one hand, Sarah settled onto Marquez's shoulders. "Wow," she murmured.

"Having a good time?" Diana asked.

Sarah nodded. Diana made a mental note to buy her a new lamb. Her old one was falling apart, leaking stuffing from his front right foot.

"Was that Austin Summer was with?" Seth asked, frowning.

Austin, his old rival. Diana took a deep breath. "She's working on some history project," she said. "She was interviewing Austin's great-uncle."

"Oh." Seth turned to Diana as if he'd suddenly remembered she existed. He leaned over and kissed her on the neck.

"Are you going to be okay with this?" she asked.

"I'm okay," he whispered. "Really."

Diana managed a smile. "Promise?"

"I told you. I'm over it. Over her." He kissed her again, a light kiss on the lips that sent a shiver of longing through her.

He looked so good, better even than she'd remembered. He'd lost a little weight—he blamed dorm food—leaving him wiry and muscular. His brown hair was shorter, and the glints from the sun had vanished. So had his Florida tan. All in all, he looked older to her, more mature. Like the college guy he was.

Until he stepped back into her life that afternoon, Diana hadn't realized how much she'd invested in Seth. All through the fall she'd told herself his letters and phone calls were just friendly updates, nothing more. She'd even considered the possibility that Seth was staying in touch with her just to find out how Summer was doing. Even now she wondered if that was the case.

"Hi, everybody." Summer finally joined the group, looking breathless and beautiful.

She and Seth locked eyes. "Well," Summer said brightly, "I guess it's time for the awkward reunion, huh?"

"Not so awkward." Seth held out his arms.

Diana knew it was a brief embrace, an old-friends embrace. Still, watching it hurt.

"You look . . . older," Summer said as she pulled away.

"Yeah. I aged about ten years during finals. You look . . ." Seth cleared his throat. "Great."

A long, awful pause followed.

"Where's Diver?" Summer asked Marquez.

"He got stuck working late at the wildlife rehab center. Something about a gator who ate one of those flamingo lawn ornaments."

Everyone laughed, but the laughter was instantly followed by another deafening silence. Finally Summer turned to Sarah. "So, you having fun, Sarah?"

"The boats have pretty lights," Sarah said.

"Have you seen our Christmas tree all lit up yet?" Summer asked.

Sarah shook her head.

"We were trying to spare the kid the trauma," Marquez said. "It'll turn her off Christmas for decades."

"They've been giving me a hard time about the tree I picked out," Summer explained to Seth.

"Remember the one your dad got last Christmas?" Seth said. "That one he picked out at the cut-your-own farm? That thing was a monster."

Against her will, Diana instantly flashed to Christmas a year ago. They'd all gotten together in Minnesota. Just a bunch of friends and family doing the holiday thing. Just an innocent get-together. Until New Year's Eve, when Diana and Seth had gotten stuck in that car and everything had changed . . .

It had started out so innocently, just a what-the-heck New Year's kiss at midnight, two old friends stuck in a funny situation they knew they'd laugh about later. But after they'd pulled away, Set had looked at her in a different way, and when he'd reached for her again and they'd kissed, it hadn't been two old friends. It had been like nothing Diana had ever felt before, not with any of the guys she'd ever dated.

It had been the kind of kiss where you lost yourself, the kind that was almost scary because you weren't sure you'd ever find yourself again if you let it go on too long.

She'd told herself it was just the illicit nature of it all. A stolen kiss. They were being bad, sneaking behind sweet Summer's back, and wasn't it kind of fun, like that first time you skipped school? She'd told herself Seth had always been just a buddy, a guy she'd never looked at that way. She'd told herself she was just feeling lost and adrift and that maybe she was just a little jealous of Summer and Seth, so much the perfect, happy couple.

But of course, she'd been lying to herself about all those things.

And now there was no Summer-and-Seth anymore. It wasn't really Diana's fault. Austin had been the real problem. Diana had just been a symptom.

Still, there were times when she wished she could make that Christmas go away. Meet Seth on her own terms, without all the history. Start fresh.

She felt a hand on her waist. "You okay?" Seth whispered in her ear.

Diana nodded. "Just reminiscing."

"Christmas does that to people," Seth said.

"Why is it I seem to remember only the bad Christmases?"

"This one'll be different," Seth promised, and for a moment Diana almost believed him.

"You comfy?" Diana asked as she tucked Sarah into bed later that evening.

Sarah nodded. She was so tiny, she practically disappeared under the comforter.

Diana set aside the *Sassy* magazine they'd been thumbing through. "Sorry about the reading material," she apologized. "It's not exactly *Goodnight Moon*. But at least you'll know how to accessorize for spring."

"You have lots of magazines." Sarah pointed to the pile on the floor.

"I believe it's vital to be up on current events. That's why I subscribe to both *Mademoiselle* and *Glamour*. It's important to entertain all points of view."

Sarah frowned.

"Okay, okay. I know I'm shallow," Diana said. "No need to rub it in. So, I guess it's time for the ol' goodnight, eh? We already did the bedtime routine. Tooth brushing, plus a good moisturizer and toner. Let's see. Want me to leave a light on?"

"Uh-huh."

"Tomorrow we'll go see Santa, since we missed him today."

"Santa isn't real."

Diana tucked her comforter around Sarah's chin. "Yeah, I've heard that rumor too. But I'm keeping an open mind. Don't you think maybe you should stop by and say hi, just in case?"

Sarah stared at her with those huge, luminous eyes. It was kind of unnerving, Diana realized. Like putting Bambi to bed.

"I mean, you were willing to give him a chance at the party, weren't you?"

"'Cause my mom said there were presents."

"Oh, I get it." Diana reached for Sarah's lamb and pushed some of the wayward stuffing back into place. "Does your lamb have a name?"

"No."

"Well, don't you think you should call him something?"

"Why?"

"I don't know. Because it's important. What if you didn't have a name? We'd have to call you Girl."

Sarah smiled a little. "I'll think about it."

"Okay. Meantime, we'll call him Lamb. You know, he could use a bath. And he's kind of oozing stuffing. Want me to sew him up?"

"No." Sarah yanked the lamb away.

"No problem. It's probably just as well. I don't really know how to sew."

"My mom doesn't either."

Diana stroked the little girl's hair. Had her own hair

ever been that silky—so smooth, it was like touching glass?

"Your mom will be back soon, Sarah. Okay?"

She didn't answer.

"She just needs a little time, is all."

"How much time?"

Diana glanced at the glowing blue numbers on her clock radio. How much? Hours? Days? Months? What if Marquez was right? What if Jennie never came back?

"You know what my mom used to say when I asked her how long? 'In two shakes of a lamb's tail.' That's pretty darn fast."

Sarah closed her eyes. Diana sat beside her for a long time. When she was sure Sarah was asleep, Diana grabbed her purse and a piece of paper on her desk.

She went to the tiny bathroom adjoining her room and closed the door gently. On the paper was her mom's itinerary, neatly typed by Mallory's assistant.

Diana pulled her cell phone from her purse, dialed the number of the Beverly Hills hotel where Mallory was staying, and sat down on the floor. While she waited for them to buzz her mom, she opened the door a crack.

Sarah was sleeping soundly. Kids looked so innocent when they were asleep.

When Mallory answered, she sounded frantic and breathless. She was on her way out with some friends.

She couldn't find her left earring, the gold one with the fake emeralds, and her nails were wet and she'd put on a zillion pounds and the zipper was stuck on her Donna Karan and how was Diana doing anyway?

Diana smiled. The first five minutes of a conversation with Mallory, you didn't have to do anything more than just utter the occasional grunt.

"I'm fine," she said. "We got a tree. Summer picked it out. It's slightly pathetic. Marquez and I did that charity thing I told you about. We sort of ended up temporarily adopting this little girl."

"Whoa. Press reverse. Run that by me again?"

She'd known that would get her mother's attention. "Just for a few days, Mallory. We're keeping her as a favor."

"Thank God. For a minute there I was afraid I was in danger of becoming a grandmother."

"We're taking her to see Santa tomorrow. Unfortunately, she's an unbeliever."

"You were that way. Highly skeptical. Probably got it from me. Ooh! Found it!"

"What?"

"My earring. In my shoe, believe it or not."

Diana could hear the sound of a closet opening. Hangers clattered as her mother rifled through her clothes.

"So what do you want for Christmas?" Mallory

asked. "I've got every boutique on Rodeo Drive at my disposal, so think big."

"Oh, you know. Whatever you get'll be fine." As long as you keep the receipts, Diana added silently. "When are you coming home, anyway?"

"January fourth, I think. I'm really sorry I can't be there, sweetie. But I'd have to jump right back on the red-eye, and it would just be crazy. And you'll have Summer and all your friends, right?"

"Yeah, we'll find something to do. We're going shopping tomorrow. I have to get this kid—Sarah's her name—some stuff." Diana paused. "Mallory, you remember that doll you gave me one Christmas? Li'l Angel Baby or Li'l Baby Angel or whatever the hell they called her?"

"Of course I remember her. You carried that plug-ugly thing around for a year. Boy, she was homely. Tabitha, wasn't that her name?"

"Actually, I had another name all picked out."

"Oh? Damn this dress is tight."

"I told you about it a zillion times. A character in one of your books, and then you forgot and—"

Diana surprised herself by the thick sound of her own voice. As if she was going to cry, almost. As if this incredibly stupid thing mattered.

"And what?" Mallory asked.

"Nothing. Look, I gotta go check on Sarah."

"Diana? You okay?"

"Fine. Never better. Good luck with the zipper. I'll call you on Christmas."

"Or I'll call you."

"Whatever. Somebody will call somebody. Have fun tonight."

Diana dropped the phone into her purse. She opened the door slowly. Sarah was curled up in a little ball, lost in a dream. Visions of sugarplums, wasn't that the deal?

Lamb had dropped to the floor. Diana picked him up and gently placed him next to Sarah. He was going to need a name, that much was certain.

10

A Kiss is Just a Kiss

Early the next afternoon Summer paused at the bottom
of the slate walkway that led to the apartment Austin
and Diver shared in the quaint older section of Coconut
Key. She'd walked all the way from her house, and now
she was regretting it. It was hot—low nineties—with a
dry, blustery wind that had whipped her hair into per-
manent tangles. She was sweaty and sandy and wilted.

Not exactly the best look for a would-be-seductress.
Which was, technically, what she was.

She stopped again near the porch, hiding behind
some bushes. She could hear muffled voices inside.
Diver would be at work, so it had to be Austin. Maybe
Austin and Esme.

Summer took a deep breath. She'd had a plan, hadn't she? The night before, as she lay wide-eyed in her bed, it had all seemed so clear. She was still in love with Austin. She couldn't get him out of her mind. She had made her resolution that morning as she sat on the empty beach watching the sun come up: She had to tell him. She planned to march on over and give him the Big Speech, the rough outlines of which were:

"I know I said I needed to be alone, but I had to prove to myself that I could get through something scary and hard like my first semester of college solo, and when I was with you again yesterday I realized I've never really stopped loving you, and now I know I can handle a relationship without getting lost in it, so would you mind getting rid of Esme and kissing me right here and now? If you don't, I may never sleep again."

Anyway, something along those lines. Maybe something with fewer commas in it.

Somehow it had sounded a lot better during the night as she tossed and turned in her hot, twisted sheets like some character in one of her aunt's romance novels.

At least she had an excuse for coming over if she chickened out on the Big Speech. She'd spent the morning tracking down Harris's long-lost love. Of course, Summer could have just called Austin with an update, but then she would have missed out on the opportunity to hide in his bushes, sweaty, dirty, and lovesick.

She wondered if she should run home and take a shower before pursuing this plan any further.

The screen door swung open before she could come to a decision. It was Esme, looking chic and sexy and definitely not sweaty.

"Summer! I thought I heard someone out here. Aus said I was hallucinating. Come on in. What are you doing lurking in the bushes? Casing the joint?"

Summer hesitated. "I'm not . . . interrupting anything?"

"Oh, no. We were in the bedroom."

"Maybe I should—"

"No, not like *that*. We're hanging in the bedroom because it's the only room with an air conditioner."

Summer followed Esme into the little bedroom. The curtains were drawn. A fan whirred near the air conditioner.

Austin was sprawled on the bed, arms behind his head. He had on a pair of cutoffs, no shirt. "Summer?" he said doubtfully.

She couldn't tell whether he was please to see her or not. Actually, he looked a little annoyed.

Esme closed the door and plopped onto the bed next to Austin. "See? It's a chilly eighty-five degrees in here. Practically arctic."

"Yeah, the weather's really been bad," Summer said lamely. She felt incredibly uncomfortable, and it wasn't just the heat.

"So what brings you to our little version of the North Pole?" Esme asked, reaching for a can of Pepsi on the nightstand.

"Maybe I should come back another time," Summer suggested.

"No, stay," Austin said. "Have a seat."

"Um, there isn't one."

"On the bed."

"Oh." Summer sat on the edge of the mattress. "Well, the thing is, I tracked down Vera. Harris's Vera."

"Already? You work fast."

"It was pretty simple. I found her sister Rose in Atlanta, the one Harris mentioned. She hadn't married, so she still had the same last name. I told her the truth, basically, about how I was doing this research paper about World War Two, and how Vera's name had come up. So she told me Vera was running a little inn, a bed-and-breakfast, on Milagro Key. That's like, I don't know, maybe twenty minutes from here, tops. Can you believe it? Anyway, she gave me Vera's number."

Austin grinned. "So what did you do with this information?"

"I called Vera, of course."

"This Pepsi's lukewarm." Esme made a point

of yawning. "I'm going to get something from the kitchen. Anybody want anything? Summer?"

"No, I'm fine."

"No, thanks, Es," Austin said.

Esme glanced from Summer to Austin, then back again. "I think maybe I'll check in with my soap. Not that this one isn't riveting." She left, closing the door behind her a little more loudly than was strictly necessary.

"She watches soap operas?" Summer whispered. "I mean, *I* do, but Esme seems too—I don't know—sophisticated."

"Yes, Esme's a strange woman."

"Are you sure it's okay I'm here? I mean, will Esme think—"

Austin waved away her concern. "Esme's not that type. Anyway, it's my bedroom," Austin said. "So did you get ahold of Vera?"

Summer barely heard his question. She was too busy trying to figure out what Austin meant. Esme wasn't *what* type? The jealous type? The paranoid type? Was Austin somehow saying that Summer, on the other hand, was that type? And anyway, what type?

"Umm . . . Summer?"

Summer shook her head, trying to reel her mind back to the present.

"Vera? Did you talk to her?"

"I did," Summer said, feeling a faint blush cover

her cheeks. "She was really cool. I didn't mention Harris. I just said I was doing this report on army nurses and I went to Carlson. And it turned out she had a cousin on the English faculty, and that sort of broke the ice."

"Didn't she wonder how you got her name?"

"I told her I was going through the history archives at the Carlson library. Fortunately, she didn't ask *which* archives. She went on and on, told me all kinds of stuff. She bought this cool little lighthouse inn with all her savings, and she loves it, but she's always short of help, and she makes these dynamite blueberry pancakes for all her guests . . . oops, I'm babbling."

"That's okay. You're cute when you babble."

Summer smiled. She felt better without Esme in the room. And Austin seemed to have relaxed a little. Still, it wasn't exactly as though she could give the Big Speech, under the circumstances.

"Here's the best part, Austin. I asked, very casually, you know, just weaving it into the conversation, if she'd had any opportunity for wartime romance. And Vera got all wistful and said yeah, there was this one handsome fellow—that's what she called him, a 'handsome fellow'—named Harris. But nothing came of it."

"Interesting."

"So very gently I asked why, and she told me she

couldn't have children, and that's why it didn't work out."

Summer smiled triumphantly, pleased at her detective work. She waited for Austin to applaud her efforts, but he just stared at the ceiling pensively.

"Austin? Don't you see? That's why Vera ran out that night. She knew she couldn't have children, and she was afraid Harris would care. I'm sure of it. And the irony is, it probably wouldn't have mattered at all. I mean, he and Louise never had children, right? Aren't you amazed I found all this out? I couldn't believe she was so open with me, especially on the phone like that. But you know how older people are. They like to talk about the past. Or maybe it's just me. Some people tell me I have that effect on them. You know, making them want to open up."

Austin just lay there, silent, frowning at the ceiling.

"Of course," Summer added, "on some people, I have precisely the opposite effect."

Austin rolled onto his side, facing her. "I'm sorry," he said, his face clouded. "I was just lost in space for a minute there. So what is it you plan to do with this data, anyway?"

"Well, get them together, naturally. I thought I'd come up with some fake reason for them to show up at the same place—that's the hard part. And then maybe even reenact the whole proposal dinner. Wouldn't that be so incredibly romantic?"

Austin just stared at her. "Summer, I really don't think that's a good idea."

"But . . . why?"

"Because Vera obviously had her reasons for running away from Harris. Maybe it was the children thing, maybe not. The point is, it's private. Not something for you to meddle in."

"But what harm could it do?" Summer asked, a little deflated. "At the very least they'll have a little reunion, talk over old times. You saw how lonely Harris was, Austin. And you could tell how much he loved her."

Austin sat up. "I don't think it's fair to Vera," he said tensely. "If she had something she didn't want to share with Harris, it's not your business to unearth it. God, that was over five decades ago! Can't you just let it rest?"

"Yesterday you weren't this upset about the idea."

"Yesterday I didn't know that Vera had a secret she didn't want revealed."

"I see."

"Besides, I thought about it last night some more, after the boat parade." Austin shrugged. "I couldn't sleep."

"Me either," Summer said, a little hopefully.

"Man, it's been hot. I always have a hard time sleeping when it's this muggy."

"Oh." She looked down at her hands, willing away the look of disappointment from her features.

"Why couldn't you sleep?" he asked.

"Um, I . . . I ate some Beefaroni before I went to bed," Summer lied. "Big mistake."

"Beefaroni at any time of the day or night is a mistake."

Summer got off the bed. She felt suddenly weary. "So you're saying no to the whole reunion plan?"

"I'm saying I think it's a lousy idea," Austin said flatly. "I'm saying sometimes people have good reasons for keeping things private. Maybe Vera was trying to protect Harris."

"Maybe. But they're in their seventies, Austin. I mean, get real. It's not like the patter of little feet is in their future." She shook her head. "I don't get why you're being such a jerk about this."

"Well, I don't get why you're pushing the whole idea so hard. He's my relative. Write your little paper and get on with your life."

"Fine," Summer said, holding up her hands. "Whatever. Sorry to bother you. I'll see myself out."

She stalked out of the room, slamming the door even harder than Esme had.

Esme was on the couch, mesmerized by a couple making out on the TV. "Leaving?" she asked.

"Oh, yeah. Definitely leaving."

Summer flung open the screen door and tromped across the lawn. To think she'd planned to come here and deliver her Big Speech! Little had she known Austin was going to behave like such a jerk.

She was almost to the corner when she heard someone running behind her. She stopped and spun around, just in time for Austin to crash right into her at a full sprint.

Austin tackled her. They went rolling onto a nicely manicured lawn.

When they landed, Summer blinked. They were lying together, a tangle of limbs on a cushion of grass.

"You okay?" Austin panted.

"Yeah. You?"

A carload of teenage boys drove by. "Go for it, dude!" one of them yelled.

"I'm fine," Austin said. "Although I'm feeling pretty depressed."

Summer yanked a piece of grass out of her hair. "Why?"

"Well, it's always kind of depressing to realize what a complete jerk you're capable of being." He gave a lopsided grin. "I don't know what I was thinking. Or maybe I do . . . I don't know. It doesn't matter."

"Austin?"

"Hmm?"

"You're not making any sense."

"Yeah. I know."

"Austin?"

"Yeah?"

"You're crushing my ribs."

"Okay, then," Austin said. "I should stop crushing you, shouldn't I? Only I was . . ."

"You were what?"

His eyes held hers. His lips were so close. His chest was pressed so hard against hers that Summer was finding it hard to breathe. She couldn't tell whether it was because she'd punctured a lung or because she felt exhilarated at being close to him again.

Austin tipped his face toward her, and suddenly their lips were touching. He was kissing her the way he had that very first time, and it didn't really matter whether she could breathe or not.

"What are you kids doing on my lawn?"

The shrieking voice forced its way into Summer's consciousness. She blinked twice before she could focus on a large, angry-looking woman wielding a broom from the porch above them.

Austin pulled away from Summer, looking confused. He jumped up, helped her to her feet, and brushed off her grass-stained knees.

"Get off my lawn, you animals!" the broom woman screeched.

Austin grabbed Summer's hand, and they hightailed

it to the safety of the sidewalk. "I'm really sorry," he said, avoiding Summer's gaze. "That was stupid. I don't know what I was thinking."

Summer was breathless, dizzy. "No, it's all right, really—"

"It isn't all right," Austin said with sudden force. "Forget it happened. It was just a kiss."

Down the block, Esme appeared on Austin's front porch. "Aus?" she called. "Everything okay?"

Austin forced himself to look at Summer. "Forget it. I already have."

She watched him run back to the house. Her lips were still wet, still buzzing, as if Austin had never left.

All in all, it was going to be a very tough kiss to forget.

11

Jingle Bells, Santa Smells . . .

"You guys get in line for Santa," Summer said that afternoon at the mini-mall. "I'm going to the mailing center to send this package to Adam."

"Want some company?" Seth asked.

Summer looked up at him in surprise. So did Marquez and Diana. "Um, sure," Summer said. "It should take only a minute."

Seth fell into step beside her. The little shopping center was filled with holiday gift buyers. "Not exactly the Mall of America, huh?" Summer said.

Seth glanced over his shoulder at Diana. "Hmm? Oh, no. Not quite."

"Why do I feel like Diana's sending laser-guided hate looks into my back?" Summer asked.

Seth laughed. "Because she is. But don't worry. She's reserving most of them for me."

A long line snaked out of the mailing center. Summer grabbed a mailing label, and they took their places at the end of the line.

"I just wanted to be alone with you for a second," Seth said while Summer filled out the label. "To tell you . . . I'm not sure, exactly. I guess to tell you that I've missed you. But I'm okay now. About us, I mean."

Summer looked up. "I'm glad, Seth. I've missed you too."

"I was thinking . . . well, it'd be nice if we could still talk from time to time." He gave a self-deprecating smile. "You know, as soon as Diana relaxes a little."

"So I'm thinking that would be maybe another decade or so?" Summer joked.

"She'll get used to everything. I hope. Let's face it, this is all pretty strange. You and me and her . . . and Austin."

He added the last name as a question. Flashing back on her strange visit to Austin's earlier that day, Summer realized she didn't really have an answer.

"Austin and I aren't . . . you know." She shrugged. "To tell you the truth, all I've had time for this semester is school. It's been great, though. Incredibly hard, but I've loved every minute of it. How about you?"

"I don't know. I don't think I'm taking to it as well as you are. Wisconsin's a big pond, and I feel like an awfully small fish, especially after high school."

"A lot of people feel that way their first year. I think it was easier for me because I was so totally afraid about going to Carlson." She laughed. "Every hour I survived was sort of a triumph. Now I really like being on my own. It's scary, but it's wonderful at the same time."

Seth smiled, that sweet smile she'd loved for so long. How strange it was that she could be here with him, talking naturally, after all that had happened between them. When they'd broken up at the end of the summer, Summer had never imagined they might actually be friends again.

"So I guess there's no room for the male species in your busy academic life?" Seth teased.

"Oh, I'm keeping an open mind," Summer said. "But I want to keep my eye on the ball too—being independent, getting my degree."

"That doesn't mean you have to join a nunnery and swear off guys."

"And how about you?"

"I don't think a nunnery would take me."

"You know what I mean," Summer said as the line slowly inched forward. "You think the long-distance romance with Diana will work?"

"It's not a romance yet," Seth said, shaking his head. "More like a really cautious flirtation. Being with Diana is sort of like dating a porcupine—you have to be real careful about the moves you make."

"An analogy I'm sure she'd appreciate."

At last they made their way to the front of the line. Summer handed her package to the clerk. "Could you send this priority? I need it to get to New England by Christmas."

"So how is ol' Adam? Or should I say Jared?" Seth asked. "You stay in touch?"

"Yeah, we write each other. Or I write and he tape-records, I should say. He still doesn't have much use of his right hand. But I think he's doing better since he moved back up to New England with his family."

"That whole thing must have been a shock for you," Seth said. "Finding out the accident victim you've been hired to take care of is really an old boyfriend."

"It wasn't so bad, really. If you watched more soap operas, Seth, you'd realize that kind of thing happens all the time."

"But that's fiction, Summer. This is real life."

She grinned. "How can you tell the difference?"

"Twelve-fifty," the clerk said as she labeled the package. Summer handed her a twenty.

"What do you buy a guy covered from head to toe

in bandages, anyway?" Seth asked. "I'm guessing he doesn't need any sunscreen."

Summer rolled her eyes. "I got him a new computer chess game. Nearly wiped out my meager savings, but I knew he'd like it. He used to slaughter me whenever we played."

The clerk handed Summer her change, and they headed back into the mall. As she tucked the bills in her purse Summer looked up to see Seth staring at her oddly.

"Why are you looking at me like that?" she asked. "Do I have something in my teeth?"

Seth rolled his eyes. "Actually, I was just thinking what a great person you are. And that I'm really glad we can still be friends."

"Great how?"

"The way you got over Adam lying to you, the way you're okay with Diana and me . . . I don't know. You don't hold grudges. You let things go. That's why you're great."

Summer took Seth's arm. "You're pretty great yourself, Seth Warner."

He looked dubious. "Think Diana will figure that out?"

"I do, actually. But just to be on the safe side, when we get near Santa, I'll let go of your arm, okay?"

Seth laughed. "Good thinking."

"Where do you think they went?" Diana asked again.

"I'm going out on a limb here and guessing the mailing center," Marquez replied.

Diana chewed on a thumbnail. "You think?"

"No, Diana. The package to Adam was just an elaborate ruse so that Summer could seduce Seth in the romantic candlelit atmosphere of Mailboxes Etcetera. Will you get a grip already?"

Diana scanned the Santa display. "Where's Sarah?"

"Right over there." Marquez pointed. "Checking out the fake elves. You know, all things considered, we were much better fake reindeer."

"Are you as tired as I am?" Diana asked. "This mommy stuff is exhausting."

"This mommy stuff sucks," Marquez corrected. "You know"—she lowered her voice—"there was a time, last summer, when I was seriously thinking that the only way I could hold on to Diver was to sleep with him. Now I'm really glad I got my act together and decided to wait. Sarah's a cute kid and all, but I'll tell you something—being around her is, like, the ultimate in birth control."

Diana laughed. "Yeah, I know what you mean. I've been chasing after her since six this morning. If I sing one more chorus of 'The Wheels on the Bus' I want you to shoot me, okay?"

"No way. Then I'd be stuck with her full time."

Diana rubbed her eyes. "You think this whole thing is crazy?"

Marquez arched one eyebrow. "Do you really want me to answer that?"

"I was kind of hoping Jennie might call or show up today. After a little time to decompress, I figured she'd come to her senses."

"Jennie isn't going to show up, Diana. And after Christmas we're going to have to do the hard thing and—"

"Shh!"

Diana knelt down as Sarah rushed over. "So, what did you think of the elves?"

Sarah shrugged. "They're not real."

"Well, no—"

"And neither is Santa."

"Still, you promised me you'd give it a shot, remember?"

"I'm going to look at the giant candy canes."

"Okay. No farther, though." Diana watcher her run off. "God, I just realized I sounded like Mallory. Now you really do have to shoot me."

They watched a little boy sob inconsolably on Santa's lap while a woman dressed as Mrs. Claus tried to snap the boy's picture.

"This really is kind of a cruel ritual, isn't it?" Marquez mused.

"Actually, Mallory never bothered with this stuff. I think it's charming . . . in a cheesy mini-mall sort of way. Hey, I was thinking that after we're done here maybe we could hit the toy store. Summer could take Sarah while we stock up on gifts. I really want to do this right."

"You're not going to get carried away, are you?"

"No." Diana smiled. "Just a few dozen toys, give or take a dozen. And she really needs some clothes."

"Diana," Marquez said seriously, "I had great Christmases, and a lot of times I was lucky to get one or two toys. One year, our first year here in the States, all I got was a box of crayons. But it was the best present I ever got."

"Okay." Diana waved her hand. "I won't overdo. Just tell me this—where do you think I could get a stuffed lamb?"

"She loves that thing. No way would she want a replacement."

"It's hemorrhaging fuzz."

Marquez nudged her. "There's Summer and Seth. Hmm. They both look a little flushed to me. . . ."

"Not funny," Diana snapped. "Not even remotely funny."

"Hey, guys," Summer called as she approached. "Looks like Sarah's next up, huh?"

Seth gave Diana a light kiss. "Miss me?"

"The real question is, did you miss me?" Diana said. It was supposed to be a joke, but even to her ears she sounded a little paranoid.

"Okay, who's next?" Mrs. Claus asked. She had a thick southern accent. Her right ear was pierced three times.

"Sarah!" Diana called.

Sarah ran over obediently. "Go on, sweetie," Diana said, herding her forward. "Say hi to Santa."

"Ho, ho, ho," Santa said in a singsong voice. "What's your name, little girl?"

"Sarah," she replied. "What's your name?"

Santa looked a little nonplussed. "Why, Santa Claus, of course!"

"I mean your *real* name. Like Sarah's my real name."

Santa sent an annoyed glance at Diana. "She's very precocious," Diana explained.

"Isn't she just?" he grumbled. Above his fake beard he had a bad patch of pimples.

"Let's get this over with, Sarah," Marquez said, stepping in. "Aunt Diana wants you to suffer the way she never had to." She lifted Sarah onto Santa's lap.

"Have you lost weight, Santa?" Marquez asked. "Lookin' good, my man. Quality time on the treadmill, eh?" She stepped back. "Santa's wearing CK One," she whispered to Diana.

"Tell Santa what you want him to bring you for

Christmas," Santa said wearily. "But here are my ground rules—no ponies, no cash, no getting rid of siblings."

"I don't want anything."

"Yeah, right," Santa chortled. "That'd be a first."

"But I don't."

Santa glared at Diana. "Don't look at me," Diana protested.

"Maybe she's not very materialistic."

"You're telling me you don't want anything?" Santa asked Sarah.

Sarah pursed her lips, deep in thought. She shook her head.

"Come on, kid," Santa whispered. "You're making me look bad here."

"Just tell Santa one thing, Sarah," Diana urged.

"Do it, kid," Marquez said. "It's your only way out of this nightmare."

"Well, there is one thing," Sarah said softly. She reached into her pants pocket and pulled out a little piece of torn paper.

"What's that?" Summer asked Diana.

"I don't have a clue. Looks like it's from a magazine."

"That's the way," Santa said, taking the picture. "Let me guess—a doll? A game? Maybe a—" He fell silent. "Kid, this is a *house!*"

"Smile and say Rudolph!" Mrs. Claus commanded, snapping Sarah's photo.

"Where'd you get that picture, Sarah?" Diana asked.

"Your magazines. It's a house for my mom and me."

Santa sent a look of pure poison at Diana. "She couldn't just ask for a dollhouse, Mom?"

"I'm not her mom."

"That's the other thing," Sarah tugged on Santa's beard, revealing a wispy brown starter mustache. "If you're really Santa, then you'll make my mom come home."

"Man, this isn't worth six-forty an hour," Santa muttered. "Okay, kid. Here's the deal. I am Santa, really I am. And I'm going to do right by you. I'm going to do my damn—my darnedest to find you a house. And your mom. Deal?"

Diana winced. "Uh, Santa? You don't want to over—" she began, but Sarah was already scampering off.

"You know what this reminds me of?" Summer said.

"A depressing scene from your Midwestern childhood?" Marquez ventured.

"No, that movie. That Santa Claus movie. We watched it last week. You know the one. *Miracle on 34th Street*. I swear, this is just like it."

"Yeah," Marquez said. "Except in that movie Santa didn't have acne."

"One other important difference," Diana added grimly. "The movie had a happy ending."

12

Laughable Kisses, and Serious Ones

"Boy, it's really coming down," Seth said that evening, standing in the doorway of the girls' house. "I'd forgotten what Florida monsoons are like. It's weird for this time of year, though."

Marquez came out of her room, sighing. "The roof is leaking again. My mattress is getting soaked."

"Seth, how about you and I move the bed out of the way?" Diver suggested.

"Does this happen often?" Seth asked.

"Only every time it rains," Diana replied as she idly channel-surfed.

"I can fix it," Seth volunteered. "I'll see about getting some shingles. My grandfather's got a ladder I can borrow."

"Meantime, I'll get a bucket," Marquez said. "And tomorrow I'll complain to our cheapskate landlord. Again."

Just then the phone rang. "I'll get it," Summer called. She reached across the kitchen table for the phone and was rewarded with a dial tone.

"That's the second time this evening," she said, carefully rearranging the piles of index cards she was preparing for her history report.

"You don't suppose it could be Jennie, do you?" Diana asked. She whispered it, even though Sarah had been in bed for hours.

"Maybe it's Santa," Marquez said as she rummaged under the sink for a bucket. "Checking to see whether Sarah would prefer a ranch or a colonial."

"That jerk. There ought to be some kind of license required for Santas," Diana muttered.

Again the phone rang. Summer groaned as she grabbed it. "Yeah?" she demanded. "Please, whoever you are. Say something. Anything."

"Man, if I'd know you were that desperate for conversation, I'd have called earlier."

"Austin?"

"Yeah. Sorry. Is it too late?"

"No, no. It's just that we've had a couple of hang-ups tonight. Hey, that wasn't you, by any chance?"

"Sorry, no. I just got home from work. Listen, I wanted to make sure I didn't offend you this afternoon with my full-body tackle."

"Offend?" Summer turned toward the wall to avoid her friends' curious stares. "No." She lowered her voice. "Not at all."

"Because it was just, like, one of those brain disconnects, you know? Esme and I were laughing about it tonight."

"She *saw* us?"

"No, but I told her all about it."

"You *told* her?"

"She said she'd done the same thing with one of her old boyfriends. A reflex kiss, I mean. Minus the tackle, of course."

Summer swallowed past a dry lump in her throat. Esme and he had gotten a good laugh out of it? Summer had half seriously considered never putting Blistex on her lips again, she'd been so blown away by Austin's kiss.

"Anyway, I wanted to tell you that if you want to go ahead with the Harris and Vera thing, I guess it's all right with me. I just don't think you should expect too much. Or push too hard."

"Well, there is one thing you could help me with."

"Okay."

"Do you know anybody with a big tent?"

"A tent?"

"For re-creating their Christmas Eve."

"Summer, I think maybe that would fall into the category of pushing too hard," Austin said.

"I know this will work. I have instincts."

"Why don't you just, I don't know, give Harris Vera's number and let nature take its course?"

"You do not have a romantic bone in your body, are you aware of that?" Summer snapped.

"Okay, okay, I surrender to your womanly instincts. There's a guy at work who does a lot of backpacking and stuff. I'll check with him on the tent."

"I'd appreciate it."

"How are you going to get them together, though?"

"I have a plan," Summer lied. "Now, I really should go. I have to work on my history paper."

"Okay. So no hard feelings, right?"

"Oh, no," Summer said frostily. "And for the record, I also found your kiss laughable."

She slammed down the phone. When she turned around, Marquez and Diana were very busy pretending they hadn't been listening.

"Show's over," Summer said.

Diana winked at Marquez. "Denial," she whispered. "Just like we said."

"I love the beach after it rains," Diana said. "It's like everything's brand-new."

Seth took her hand. It was almost midnight. They walked in silence at the surf's edge, both barefoot. The wet sand was packed tight, cool and unyielding under their toes. The air smelled briny and alive. On the horizon a few clouds had parted, revealing a light dusting of pale stars, but the moon was hidden from view. Without the moonlight glazing the waves, the ocean was an invisible, vast presence. It was pure sound, the soothing crash and tumble of waves and nothing more.

"There's no moon tonight," Diana said.

"Just because we can't see it doesn't mean it's not there."

"Can I ask you something without sounding jealous and paranoid and just generally neurotic?" Diana said.

"Well, it would be a first," Seth said affectionately, "but hey, give it a shot."

"What did you and Summer talk about at the mall today?"

"The usual stuff. School, Christmas. Let's see. Oh, we talked about Adam a little." Seth paused. "And I told Summer I hoped we could be friends."

Diana let her hand slip out of Seth's "What does that mean, exactly?"

"You know, Diana. A friend. Someone to bum

money from. Someone to watch TV with. Someone who'll pick you up when your car blows a gasket. A friend."

"I guess I don't see . . ." Diana stopped walking. The cool water rushed over her toes. "I guess I don't see why you have to see her anymore at all. Why it can't just be over totally."

Even in the dark, she could see Seth's exasperated expression. She couldn't really blame him. But she couldn't seem to help herself either.

"It can't be totally over," Seth said, placing his hands on her shoulders, "because I care about Summer. I always will. You can't just turn feelings on and off like a faucet, Diana. I've known Summer a long time. I hope she's always my friend."

He cupped her face in his hands and gently kissed her. It was a tender, soft kiss, and she knew it was meant to reassure her. But all Diana could think of was the hundreds, maybe thousands, of times he'd kissed Summer, and how that memory would always be there, ruining moments such as this.

She pulled away abruptly. "I just don't know if I can deal with all the history, Seth. The lies and anger and everything."

Seth smiled wryly. "Nobody lied more last summer than you, Diana."

"True. But that's part of the problem. I know it's

my own fault, but I wonder if you can ever look at me and see *me*. Not the person who broke up you and Summer."

"You didn't break us up." Seth gave a short laugh. "Well, you didn't help, God knows. But the truth is, even Austin didn't break us up. The problem was between Summer and me. It just wasn't . . . working out."

They resumed walking. After a while Seth took Diana's hand again. She tried to enjoy the moment: the cool sand, the salt breeze, the feel of Seth's warm fingers twining in hers, the sound of his steady breathing.

But she couldn't. All she could do was imagine another night not so far in the future—a night when she'd have to walk alone on this same beach without Seth. A night when she'd know she'd lost him to Summer for good.

"Sometimes I wish I could just erase the past," Diana said. "Get amnesia, maybe. I wouldn't have to forget everything. Just the hard stuff. The stuff that hurts. The times I've disappointed people. The times people have disappointed me."

"Are you talking about me?"

"No." Diana shrugged. "You haven't, not yet. I don't know who I mean. Mallory. Other guys. Just . . . people."

"If you lost all the bad stuff, the good stuff wouldn't feel so good," Seth said.

He paused, pulling her close. Diana laid her head on his shoulder, gazing out at the ocean, as invisible and mysterious as her future.

"We can't wish our past away, Diana," Seth whispered. "But maybe we can learn from it. Maybe you and I can find something Summer and I couldn't find. Maybe we can find a way to make things work."

They kissed again, long and slow. When Diana opened her eyes, she could just make out the moon glowing small and yellow, like a porch light on a foggy night.

13

Spoonbills and Stuffed Lambs

Two days later Summer was on the porch sorting through some recent purchases when she heard Austin's car rattling up the drive.

Esme was in the front seat with him. She waited in the car while Austin removed yellow canvas and a large bundle of poles from the trunk.

"I come bearing gifts," Austin called as he strode up the drive. He dropped the bundle at Summer's feet.

"Is that a tent?" Summer asked.

"It's a potential tent, anyway."

"Khaki would have been more realistic. But I'll take what I can get."

"What's in the big box?" Austin asked.

"Stuff," Summer said evasively.

"Is that a canteen I see?"

Summer shoved the cardboard box toward him. "See for yourself. But if you don't approve, just do me a favor and keep your mouth shut. I'm starting to have second thoughts as it is."

"Two mess kits, an army blanket, a nurse's cap, a helmet." Austin whistled. "Where did you find all this?"

"Mostly the Goodwill outlet and that army surplus store up the highway."

Austin shook his head. "So you're really going through with this reunion?"

"I'm not sure anymore." Summer yanked the box away. "It seemed like such a good idea at first, but then I started to have doubts when you were so dead set against it. And when I told Marquez and Diana about it, they just sort of rolled their eyes and said I was an incurable romantic. Well, Diana said I was an incurable romantic. Marquez said I was deranged."

Austin frowned. "I went to all the trouble of finding you this tent," he said. "Now I sort of feel let down."

"You told me this idea was dumb."

"I know, but I figured you'd barrel ahead with it anyway. You are incredibly stubborn, in case no one's ever pointed that out to you. And anyway, I brought you the tent, didn't I?"

"I don't know what to do." Summer sighed. "I

guess I'll see how I feel. Tomorrow's Christmas Eve, so this'll have to wait till after the holidays. There's no way I could get them together tomorrow. Even if I *did* think of a way to do it."

Esme honked the horn impatiently. "Hang on, Es," Austin called. He turned back to Summer. "Finished with your paper?" he asked.

"Almost. But I'm not sure how to end it. I guess I was waiting to see if I'd go through with this plan." She smiled wistfully. "I even got a CD. Greatest hits of the forties. They're kind of cool, actually. There's this one song, 'I'll Be Seeing You.' They used to play it all the time during the war. Really sad."

"I've heard it. Harris has some old, worn record he used to play. 'I'll be seeing you in all the old familiar places . . .'"

"That's the one."

"Yeah, it is sad, when you think about all the men and women who died. All the couples who were never reunited."

Another car, even more rust-eaten than Austin's, rolled up. Diver jumped out and waved to Summer and Austin.

"You know, I could stick around if you want," Austin said. "That tent's tough to put up. Especially with this wind. Weather sure has been freaky lately."

"I'll manage."

"It might require some manly brute strength."

"The same could be said of Esme," Summer replied coolly. "Besides, I can get Diver to help. And Seth's coming over later to work on our roof. You'd better hit the road."

"Look, if you do go ahead with your plan, call me, okay?"

"Sure."

Austin started to leave, then hesitated. "You know, you were wrong about what you said the other day. I *do* have a romantic bone in my body." He grinned. "I'm thinking it may be my left tibia, but I'd need an X ray to verify it."

Summer crossed her arms over her chest. "Whatever you say."

"If you read some of my latest poetry, you'd believe me."

"Odes to Esme?"

Austin's smile faded. He looked as though he was about to say something, then reconsidered. "I've been working on another subject, actually."

"What?"

"Oh, you know how poets are. We don't like to discuss works in progress."

"When will you be done with it?"

"I don't know," Austin said, and he suddenly looked terribly sad. "Maybe never."

Summer watched Austin head back to his car. He passed Diver on the way, acknowledging him with a terse nod.

"What's up with Austin?" Diver asked.

"You tell me. You're his roommate."

Diver sat on the steps. "I told you. We don't discuss our feelings."

"I forgot." Summer sighed. "Just your gaskets, right?"

"Carburetors. What's the tent for?"

"I'm not sure."

Diver leaned back, face raised to the sun. "Marquez back from her lunch shift?"

"Yeah. She and Sarah are building sand castles down on the beach. At least, Marquez is. Sarah's kind of just observing."

"Summer? Everything okay? You look a little confused."

Summer sat down beside her brother. "I am. Austin's confusing me. My history project's confusing me. I guess you could pretty much say life is confusing me. How come you never seem confused, Diver?"

He smiled at her. "Because I accept my confusion instead of fighting it. It's easier that way."

"Does Marquez ever confuse you?"

Diver laughed. "Every day. But that's okay. I love her. So I figure the confusion is the price I have to pay to be in love. It seems like a fair trade-off. It's just one of the mysteries of life. I like it that way."

"I wish I did."

Diver kicked off his shoes and stretched out his legs. "Today at work we had this great mystery."

Summer smiled. Diver's job guaranteed he always had some strange new alligator or pelican story to tell.

"A lady came in this morning with this Kleenex box filled with six baby birds. She'd found the mother nearby. It looked like maybe a cat or a dog had killed her. I could tell right away they were roseate spoonbills, this really rare species. Cool, right?"

"Right."

"So I put them under the warming lamp. But the whole time my boss is freaking out because there are six of these birds, when everybody knows a spoonbill will lay two or three eggs at the most."

"Any third-grader knows that," Summer said, grinning.

"So I finally told Hal just to go with it, that it's a mystery, but that in the meantime I could use some help." Diver frowned. "Did this story have a point? I've sort of forgotten."

"I love your *Animal Planet* stories," Summer said. "It doesn't really matter whether they have a point or . . ." Summer stopped. A brilliant idea had just popped into her brain, squeezing out every other thought. "Diver, these spoon birds are rare, right?"

"Spoonbills. In the old days they used to kill them and use their feathers for women's hats. They're protected now, though."

"So these sextuplets would be a major draw, right?"

"If you're into birds, sure."

Summer leapt up. "Diver, I am suddenly less confused. About one thing, anyway. And I have you to thank for it."

"You're welcome, I guess." Diver looked up at her, squinting into the sunlight. "So how come I'm more confused?"

"Just one of the mysteries of the universe," Summer said happily.

Diana jumped when Summer threw open her bedroom door. "Jeez! I was afraid you were Sarah," she said, hand to her heart. "Quick, close the door. She's still playing with Marquez, right?"

Summer made her way through the minefield of unwrapped toys spread over Diana's floor. "Well, playing might be pushing it. She's been awfully subdued today, have you noticed?"

"I know. I'm worried about her."

"Want me to help wrap?"

"If you want," Diana said tersely.

"Are you mad at me about something, Diana?"

"No. Why?"

"You've just seemed kind of standoffish the past couple of days. Distant."

"I've got a lot on my mind," Diana said. "Sarah and all that."

"And Seth?"

Diana curled a long piece of ribbon with the edge of her scissors. "And Seth."

"There's nothing between Seth and me anymore," Summer said. "You've got to believe that, Diana, or you two aren't going to have a chance."

"I'm supposed to believe you're rooting for us?"

"I am. I love you both. I'm not saying it isn't weird seeing you together. But I do want things to work out for you two."

"I wish I could believe that," Diana said softly. "I *want* to believe it, but . . . it's so hard. After everything that's happened between us. I thought I could handle it better. I was wrong."

Summer grabbed a roll of snowman wrapping paper. "I'm going to tell you something I haven't told anyone, okay? I still have . . . feelings . . . for Austin."

"Wow, breaking news. Alert CNN," Diana said in a deadpan voice. "Marquez and I have been telling you that for weeks. What are you, oxygen-deprived? Is your brain even functioning?"

"Well, if you think that already, why are you worried about Seth and me?"

Diana shrugged. "How can I know how things'll end up with you and Austin? Even you don't know. Besides, Seth was your first love, Summer. You never get over your first love."

"Sure you do." Summer hesitated. "If your second love is the one you want to last forever."

Diana was surprised to see tears in Summer's eyes. "Is that what Austin is?"

"Maybe. But I don't think he feels the same way about me anymore. If he ever did. I know that's not what you want to hear. But it's the truth." She paused. "And it's also the truth that Seth and I are over for good. Okay?"

Diana gave a small smile. "Okay. Thanks, Summer." She tossed a roll of ribbon. "Here. Make yourself useful."

Summer reached for the stuffed lamb Diana had bought for Sarah. "Cute."

"Marquez doesn't think so. She says Lamb is irreplaceable. I say he's a health hazard."

Summer found a pair of scissors on the floor and cut out a large square from the roll of snowman paper.

"Listen, I may need your help tomorrow for a little while."

"You're going ahead with the big World War Two reunion?"

"You think I'm crazy, don't you?"

Diana sighed. "There was a time when I might have said you were crazy, yes. But a few days ago I became an adoptive mother while wearing a reindeer suit. It's the people-in-glass-houses syndrome. I no longer feel I am in a position to call anyone crazy."

"It'll be okay, Diana. Sarah's mom could still show up."

"We haven't had any more hang-up calls. That was my one hope—that Jennie was just working up her nerve."

"Tomorrow's Christmas Eve. Maybe that will bring her around. Holidays make people all sentimental."

"Maybe."

"It could happen."

"Yeah, and while we're being optimists, maybe Santa will drop a three-bedroom house down our chimney."

"We don't have a chimney," Summer pointed out.

"You see what I'm up against."

Summer taped the corners and tied a bow around the stuffed lamb's box. "You never know, Diana. Christmas is a time for miracles."

"I cannot believe you are capable of saying things like that out loud." Diana rolled her eyes. "Next year I'm suspending your Netflix subscription for the month of December. No more Christmas movies for you, girl."

14

Under the Big Top

"Who called a few minutes ago, Summer?" Diana asked early the next afternoon. "And why are you staring at the telephone like it's armed with nuclear warheads?"

"Am not."

"Are too. That isn't fear I see on your face?"

"No," Summer said defensively. "It's indecision."

"Call him, Summer," Marquez advised from the living room, where she was busy shaking gifts to determine their contents.

"That last call was a wrong number, Diana," Summer said, pointedly ignoring Marquez. "They wanted a Joe something."

"Was it a girl?" Diana asked.

"Yeah. But—"

"It could have been Jennie," Diana whispered, glancing over at her bedroom, where Sarah was napping.

"I don't think so, Diana," Summer said gently.

Diana flopped into a kitchen chair dejectedly. "Well, at least your crazy idea is picking up steam. When are Harris and Vera coming?"

"Another hour, probably. Assuming they really come. Thanks, you guys, for all your help setting up the tent." Summer checked her watch. "I hope they get here before it starts to rain."

"*I* hope Seth gets around to fixing the roof before it storms," Diana said. "He only got about a quarter of the shingles replaced before he ran out yesterday."

"I called our beloved landlord again," Marquez said. "He said, 'Screw you and have a merry Christmas.'"

"That would explain our reasonable rent," Diana said.

Summer gazed out the window and sighed. All day clouds had been rolling in, darkening the sky ominously. "You know, I've almost accepted the fact that this Christmas is going to be snowless. But come on, thunderstorms? That's just adding insult to injury."

"She's stalling," Diana said to Marquez.

"Call him, Summer," Marquez instructed.

"He's probably out with Esme, anyway. Doing last minute shopping or something."

"Call him, Summer," Diana said softly. "You know you want to."

"I'm thinking about it, okay?"

Marquez held up a package that had been delivered that morning. "Diana, what do you figure this FedEx package from your mom is? Maybe some matching mother–daughter diamonds? Another gold card?"

Diana shrugged. "Search me."

"Want me to open it for you?"

"Marquez!" Summer scolded. "It's only Christmas Eve."

"I was just trying to eliminate the suspense. Besides, we opened my mom's cookies." She shook the box again. "Let me put it this way—how guilty was your mom feeling about missing Christmas?"

"Mallory is immune to guilt. She says it gives her frown lines." Diana nudged Summer with her foot. "Call him, already."

"What if the reunion works out great, Summer?" Marquez said. "Austin would want to be here."

"And every minute he's here," Diana added, "is a minute he's not with Esme."

Summer picked up the phone, then set it down. "Let me ask you both something. And I do not want you to laugh. I don't even want you to slightly smirk.

Has a guy ever told either of you that he found your kissing . . . laughable?"

"Not in so many words," Diana said, the corners of her mouth twitching.

"Negative on that," Marquez reported, covering her mouth.

"If a guy did say something along those lines, would you take it as a bad sign?"

Diana took a deep breath. Marquez snorted.

"Call him, Summer," Diana managed to say.

Summer punched in Austin's number before she could think of all the reasons not to. By the time Austin answered, she could barely hear her voice over the howls of her roommates.

"Very impressive," Austin said as he stepped inside the yellow tent a half-hour later. "I like the 1944 calendar. Nice touch."

"It's not original, actually. I typeset it on my computer."

Summer clicked on the iPod speakers in the corner. Soft big band music began to play. "I have the speakers sort of camouflaged by the army blanket," she said. "Didn't want the high-tech stuff to spoil the mood."

"I particularly like the table setting. Candles, mess kits, cans of pork and beans."

"That's just for effect, since I couldn't find any C-rations. I figured Diana and Marquez and I would fix them dinner. If, you know, things go well." The tent shuddered in the wind, "I hope we've got this thing nailed down okay," Summer said. "It looks like it's going to be a big storm."

Austin sat in one of the folding camp chairs Summer had borrowed from a neighbor. "I can't believe you got Harris and Vera to come. On Christmas Eve, no less. It boggles the mind, Summer."

"I have Diver to thank for that." Summer laughed. "It was pretty amazing, Austin. First I called Vera, then Harris. I told them each how I remembered they were into bird-watching and how my brother had discovered this nest of six roseate spoonbills in our yard, and they both completely freaked. I guess for a birder that's like winning the lottery. I gave them directions, and Harris said he'd be here right away."

"And Vera?"

"Her I'm not so sure about. The bed-and-breakfast she runs is full, and she had to wait for her manager to get there and take over. She didn't sound all that sure she could get away." Summer rubbed her eyes. "God, Austin, what if she doesn't come?"

"Have faith. You've gotten this far with this ridiculous quest," he said. "I guess you failed to mention the birds are actually at the wildlife center."

"A little bit of lying is permissible in the name of true love."

Austin smiled wistfully. "Is it?"

Summer studied him for a moment, unsure of the meaning of his smile. "Sure. Haven't you ever lied to Esme?"

"No. I've never needed to with her."

"How about with me? In the old days, I mean?"

Austin didn't answer.

"So you *have* lied to me?" Summer asked. Her voice was light and teasing, but Austin's troubled expression made her more than a little curious.

Slowly Austin's gaze made its way to her. "If I ever did lie—and I'm taking the Fifth on this—it would have been only because I cared about you."

"Knock knock!" Marquez poked her head in the tent. "Damn, I was hoping I might be interrupting something. I think Harris is driving up! What do we do?"

Summer leapt out of her chair. "Whatever you do, don't let him near the tent until we're ready."

With Austin and Marquez on her heels, Summer ran out to greet Harris as he pulled up. "You found us!" she exclaimed as he parked the car. "I didn't expect you to get here so quickly."

Harris stepped out of the car. "Six spoonbills, my

dear. For that, even a law-abiding man breaks the speed limit."

"Hey, Harris." Austin shook his great-uncle's hand.

"Good to see you, my boy."

"And this is Marquez, one of my roommates," Summer said. "And that's Diana on the porch."

Harris gave a courtly bow. "Three lovely ladies. No wonder you're visiting, Austin."

"Well, it wasn't for the spoonbills."

"Where are they, anyway?" Harris said. He scanned the area, frowning. "This seems like quite an unlikely place for a nesting site."

"But then, they're an unlikely family," Summer said quickly. "What with being sextuplets and all."

"Still, spoonbills are found in colonies, usually near mangroves. No, this just doesn't seem right at all. . . ."

Summer smiled lamely. "Hey, Christmas is a time for miracles, Harris."

A car approached, and Summer's heart skipped a couple of beats. Could it be Vera already?

But it was just Seth, driving up in his grandfather's station wagon. A ladder was strapped to the top.

"That's Seth," Summer told Harris, barely hiding her disappointment. "He's an old, uh, friend of mine. From Wisconsin."

Seth jumped out of the car. "Hey, I found some more shingles, can you believe it? Laskin's Hardware was actually open on Christmas Eve!"

Suddenly he froze, eyes on Austin. "Oh," he said quietly. "Hey, Austin."

"Seth." Austin nodded. "How've you been?"

"Not bad."

Summer cleared her throat. "Seth, this is Harris, Austin's great-uncle."

"Nice to meet you, sir." Seth shook his hand.

Diana walked over and gave Seth a kiss. "I'm not sure you should do any more work on the roof," she said. "It's going to storm soon. You'll turn into a lightning rod."

"Relax. I'll be careful."

"Speaking of storms," Harris said, "I should really take a look at these marvelous specimens and be on my way. I don't want to get stuck in a gully-washer."

"Specimens?" Seth repeated.

"Birds," Summer said.

"Not just any birds." Harris shook a finger at her. "Roseate spoonbills. Why don't you point me in the right direction, Summer, dear?"

Summer's heart was doing a nice little reggae number. How long could she stall him? What if Vera didn't come at all? What if Austin was right and this was the most incredibly stupid idea she'd ever had in her life?

"Why don't you take a quick tour of the house?" Marquez suggested.

"I'd love to—Marquez, was it? But first things first. I cannot wait another minute to see my spoonbills."

All eyes were on Summer. She swallowed hard. Suddenly, looking into Harris's sweet, hopeful eyes, she had the awful feeling that Vera was never going to come. This was not a time for miracles. This was Christmas in Florida, where it never snowed and people put lights on palm trees.

"Harris, the thing is," Summer said slowly, "the birds aren't exactly right here."

"Oh?"

"No, they're somewhere else,"

"Where, then?" he asked.

"Well, that's a long story. . . ."

Austin elbowed her hard. She looked at him. He jerked his head.

Both Summer and Harris turned. An old white Cadillac was coming up the driveway.

"A friend?" Harris inquired.

"That's what I'm hoping," Summer said, crossing her fingers.

They watched as the car stopped. The front door

slowly opened. Out stepped a striking woman, frail but elegant. Her white hair was caught up in a bun.

As she closed the car door her gaze fell on Harris. She stood very still, a quizzical expression on her delicate face.

Harris was frozen for a long moment. At last he took a step toward her. His hand was outstretched, as if he were reaching for a mirage. His fingers were trembling.

Summer felt goose bumps fan out over her body. She realized she wasn't breathing.

Neither Harris nor Vera moved. Vera's chin trembled. Summer could see the tears in her eyes threatening to spill over.

Summer watched in terror. The suspense was unbearable. Were those tears of joy or sadness? Was Harris trembling out of happiness or fear?

"Harris?" Vera whispered.

"Vera."

Silence. Nothing.

No passionate embrace. No movement at all.

She'd blown it.

"Maybe you, uh, would like to . . . uh, sit . . . ," Summer mumbled.

Nothing. No response.

"Harris," Austin said gently. "The tent. Why don't you go ahead and talk to Vera there?"

Harris blinked, as if awakened from a trance. He nodded. His expression was grim.

He approached Vera stiffly, arm outstretched.

She hesitated, then took his arm. Together they walked slowly toward the little yellow tent.

Neither said a word.

15

I'm Dreaming of a Wet Christmas . . .

Summer gazed dejectedly out the window at the tor-
rential downpour. The little yellow tent was barely
visible. "Harris and Vera have been in there two and a
half hours," she said. "I can't stand it any longer."

"They must have hit it off or they wouldn't be sitting in that pathetic tent," Marquez pointed out. "I'm
surprised it hasn't blown away yet."

"They could be arguing," Summer said. "Or waiting out the storm. Or . . . or crying."

"Or doing it," Seth volunteered, earning a
ferocious glare from Austin.

"Seth!" Diana scolded. "Keep it G-rated. We have
a kid in the house."

"Where is Sarah, anyway?" Summer asked.

"In my bedroom, reading *Seventeen*. Maybe I should let her open that Dr. Seuss book early. She did ask me when Santa was bringing her mom, and I just didn't know—" Diana was interrupted by a sharp crack of thunder. "I told her sometimes Santa gets caught in traffic, so it might be a while."

"Crap. There's a new leak in the kitchen," Marquez reported, grabbing the mop. "That makes four total. We're out of buckets."

"This is my fault," Seth said. "If I'd gotten hold of those shingles sooner, I could have fixed more of the roof."

"Seth," Summer chided, "you're not exactly the resident handyman. It's not your fault we rent from a slumlord."

Sarah appeared in the bedroom doorway. "It's raining in the bedroom," she said softly.

"Wonderful." Summer groaned. "I swear, it's so dark out there, it could be night. Is this, like, the worst Christmas in history or what?"

Diver patted her on the back. "No way, Summer."

"Yeah, maybe you're right. It's the worse Christmas *Eve* in history."

Summer turned to Austin, who was sitting on the couch, staring at the TV. *White Christmas* was on without sound. At the bottom of the screen was a notice that the National Weather Service had posted a severe thunderstorm warning.

"Austin, what do you think?" Summer asked. "Should I go check on them again?"

"You already tried to eavesdrop on them once, Summer. You're never going to hear them over the thunder. Why don't you just chill out? They're grown-ups."

A blinding flash of lightning lit the dark sky, followed by thunder so loud the walls shook. Sarah ran into Diana's arms, sobbing. The lights blinked twice, then went off, plunging the house into darkness. The TV went dead.

"Great," Austin muttered. "Now I'll never know how it ends."

"It snows and everybody lives happily ever after," Summer said. "Unlike real life."

"I can't see a thing," Marquez muttered. "Where did we put those emergency candles?"

"Harris and Vera have them."

"You guys have a flashlight, at least?" Seth asked.

"Well, sort of," Summer replied. "We have one, but I had to borrow the batteries for the iPod speakers."

"Which is where?" Seth asked.

"With Harris and Vera."

"I'm thinking maybe it's time to check up on our lovebirds," Marquez said.

"What if they're really mad at me?" Summer asked.

"I'll check the circuit breakers first," Seth volunteered. "Where are they?"

"In Diana's closet," Marquez said. "But you're never going to be able to see anything, it's so dark."

"I have an idea." With Sarah clinging to her hand, Diana went to her room. She returned with her Rudolph head. The red nose glowed brightly in the pitch-dark living room. "Follow me, Seth."

"Once again," Austin mused, "life imitates art."

As Diana led Seth away there was a knock at the front door, barely audible over the howling storm. "Oh, God. It's them," Summer said.

She threw open the door. Two small, wet figures stood huddled on the porch. "May we?" Harris inquired.

"Please, come in," Summer cried. "Look at you both! You're soaked."

She closed the door behind them. They stood side by side in the shadows, their faces barely visible in the occasional flash of lightning.

Everyone fell silent. The only sound was the rain, drumming on the roof and dripping musically into the buckets.

"You must be Summer," Vera whispered.

Summer nodded, stepping closer. Vera looked very old and very frail. Worse yet, she looked terribly sad.

What had Summer been thinking, playing with the emotions of an old woman this way? How could she have been so callous?

"Whose idea was this . . . this reunion?" Vera asked. Summer had to strain to hear her over the rain.

Summer felt as though she was going to cry. "It was all mine. Austin and Harris had nothing to with it. I'm sorry," she said, her throat tight. "I don't know what I was thinking. I had no right. . . ."

"You misguided girl," Vera said, her voice breaking. Tears rolled down her cheeks. "You silly fool, meddling in the lives of two old people, playing with their feelings"

Summer bit her lip. "I'm so very sorry, Vera."

Sobbing, Vera moved toward Summer, her hand raised. Summer tensed, waiting for the slap she knew was coming. The slap she deserved.

"Vera, Summer meant well," Austin interjected. "She just wanted—"

The hand came down. It rested on Summer's shoulder. Gently Vera pulled Summer close.

"You dear, silly child," she whispered. "How am I ever going to thank you?"

As she pulled blankets from her bed to wrap around Harris and Vera, Summer found herself laughing with relief. They weren't mad. They really weren't mad.

They were grateful to her. Harris had told her so again and again.

She bunched up the blankets and went back into the living room, where they were huddled in the darkness. She presented them to Harris, who gallantly wrapped a soft quilt around Vera's shoulders.

Summer sighed and sat down on the floor, trying to relax her stiff muscles.

"Are you all right, dear?" Harris asked.

"I'm fine. It's just . . . you and Vera were in there so long . . . I was so afraid."

"We were dancing," Vera explained. "We must have played 'I'll Be Seeing You' a dozen times. That was our song, you see."

Another shot of lightning tore the sky. A slow, awful cracking sound followed. A moment later the horrendous noise of splintering wood and shattering glass came from the direction of Diana's bedroom.

Diana, Seth, and Sarah sprinted out of the room. "Whoa! We have a major problem!" Seth reported.

"There's a tree in the bedroom!" Sarah cried.

"Lightning," Diana added breathlessly. "A branch of that pine broke off and went through the window. It's extremely wet back there. I'm going to have to buy a whole new wardrobe."

"There's not much we can do to fix it until the storm passes," Seth said.

"This will never do," Vera said. "Come with me and I'll put you up at my bed-and-breakfast for the night. It's just twenty minutes down the road."

"The highway could be flooded," Seth pointed out.

"Not any worse than this house," Vera replied. "I will not take no for an answer. You'll be my guests for Christmas. It's the least I can do to repay you for your kindness."

Summer grinned. "Well, we sure can't stay here."

"Austin and I can just head on back to the apartment," Diver said.

"And leave me stranded alone on Christmas Eve?" Marquez cried. "No way!"

"Austin, how about you?" Harris asked.

"He probably has plans with Esme, Harris," Summer said.

Austin shook his head. "She's spending Christmas morning with her parents."

"Come on, my boy," Harris urged. "I'd like to have some family around for a change."

"I just need to move some of my stuff into garbage bags so it doesn't get any wetter," Diana said. "And we can't forget to bring the presents."

"We'll take two cars," Vera instructed. "Why don't one of you youngsters drive my Cadillac? I'm not much for driving in this weather."

Seth cleared his throat. "Um, I hate to blow the

party mood, but I need to head on back to town. My grandfather . . . I should be with him."

"Seth!" Diana cried. "Your aunt Carol's there. She'll be with him. And it's just for the night. You can drive back first thing Christmas morning."

"I have to, Diana. It's . . . you know, a family thing. You and Sarah could come over to his house, but it's packed already."

"Right," Diana snapped. "Sure. Family comes first." She shot a glance at Summer. "Somebody else will always come first."

Seth sighed. "There'll be other Christmases."

"Yeah, I know. Mallory used to tell me that all the time."

"This is not the same thing."

"Fine, Seth." Diana held up her hands. "Forget about it."

Sarah tugged on Diana's arm. "Will Santa know where to find us now?"

Diana's lower lip trembled. She took a deep breath. "I hope so, hon," she said softly. "But don't count on it, okay?" She cast a dark look at Seth. "He has his good years and his bad years."

16

Gifts

"I feel just terrible about this," Vera said again that evening. "I had no way of knowing my manager was going to rent out those last rooms while I was away, of course. But you weren't the only people put out by the storm. . . ." She wrung her hands. "And to have you end up here in the stable, of all places! Can you ever forgive me?"

"Vera, this is great," Summer assured her. "To begin with, you fed us a fantastic dinner. And we've got all the comforts of home here."

"Still, Vera fretted, "this is hardly my idea of hospitality."

"Hmm," Austin said, tapping his finger to his

chin. "Let's add this up. There's no room at the inn. We're stuck in a manger on Christmas Eve—"

"I think we can all see where you're heading, Austin," Marquez interrupted. "Trust me. The casting's all wrong."

"Let's see. You have cots, sleeping bags, pillows," Vera said, ticking the items off on her fingers. "And, of course, the scintillating company of our resident mare. The rain's slowing a bit, but it's so chilly. You think you'll be warm enough?"

"Stop your worrying, Vera," Harris said. "They're kids. They're tough."

"I suppose so. Well, good night, then," Vera said. She knelt down beside Sarah. "You sleep tight, sweetie,"

"Does Santa ever come here?" Sarah asked.

"Every year, like clockwork." Vera patted Sarah's head gently. "Now, you try to get some sleep."

"I've never slept with a horse before."

"She hardly ever snores, I promise. Would you like me to bring you one more cookie before you go to sleep?" Vera asked.

"But she already brushed her teeth," Marquez objected. Her hand flew to her mouth. "Oh, man, did I just say that? The mother disease. It's catching! Somebody kill me before I nag again."

"I'll go back to the kitchen with you, Vera," Summer volunteered. "Save you the trip."

Sheltered by an umbrella, Harris, Vera, and Summer headed back to the inn. It was a charming old lighthouse on a small, underdeveloped key, half of which was a wildlife preserve.

The main house, a simple white Victorian, featured eight guest rooms, a cozy parlor, and a wide screened porch that overlooked the water.

"That rain is like ice," Summer said as she stepped into Vera's warm kitchen.

"Remarkable weather, yes," Vera said. "But then"—she smiled at Harris—"it's been a remarkable day all the way around, hasn't it?" She straightened her dress. "I suppose I should see to my other guests. You help yourself to the cookies, Summer."

Harris took a seat at the antique oak table in the center of the kitchen. "Can you spare me a minute?" he asked.

"Of course," Summer said, joining him.

"I just wanted to—" Harris cleared his throat. "To thank you for your crazy scheme. If it hadn't been for you, Vera and I might never have seen past our own stubbornness. I shouldn't have let her go so easily. I was a fool. And so was Vera, come to think of it. I guess she told you the reason she vanished all those years ago." He took off his glasses, wiping them with a white handkerchief. "As if that would have mattered! But that's all water under the bridge, isn't it?"

"I'm just glad it worked out, Harris. I take it this means you'll be . . . seeing each other again?"

Harris gave a sly grin. He pulled out his wallet. Behind his license was a piece of gray string, tied into a small circle.

"The ring? The one you—"

"Tomorrow I intend to ask Vera for her hand in marriage," Harris whispered.

Summer tried not to show her surprise. "Don't you think maybe that's a little bit, um, fast?"

Harris laughed as he put the string away. "You should have seen the shock on your face just now. Maybe it's true that youth is wasted on the young. You're so careful sometimes, as if you have all the time in the world. . . ." He shrugged. "Anyway, we shall see what we shall see. What's the worst that can happen? She can't exactly run off this time."

"Did you tell Austin yet?"

"No." Harris pursed his lips. "He's rather cautious at heart. I doubt he'd approve."

Summer nodded. "You're probably right. He didn't think my scheme to reunite you and Vera was such a hot idea either."

"He's a wonderful boy, Austin. But occasionally thoroughly wrongheaded." Harris looked at Summer, smiling that same half smile she used to think belonged to Austin alone. "I shouldn't ask you this. Feel free to tell me I'm a nosy old man and to go to hell."

"After all the questions I asked you for my inter-view? I owe you."

"Are you . . . are you in love with Austin?"

"Yes," Summer said simply. She was surprised at how easily the answer came to her lips.

"I thought as much."

"But I don't think he feels the same way about me."

Harris pushed back his chair. He walked to the window over the kitchen sink, hands clasped behind his back. The rain beat softy, relentlessly.

"There's a reason Austin is keeping his distance from you, Summer," Harris said, his back to her.

"Esme?"

He gave a short laugh. "No. Esme is just a distrac-tion. A diversionary tactic. I suspect he wants no more from her than what she wants from him."

"She's some diversion."

"I'm going to tell you something now," Harris said. "It's not my place. I probably shouldn't. But today, thanks to you, I'm feeling like all things are possible. And that is a gift that I would like to try to return."

Slowly Harris turned to face her. His eyes were wet and filled with an awful, desperate pain. "It's about Austin and about Austin's dad."

Summer felt a cold knot tighten in her chest. She thought of the times Austin had talked about his dad, of how unreachable and alone he had always seemed at those moments. She thought of the terrified look she'd seen in his eyes.

"About his dad's disease," Summer said slowly. It wasn't really a question.

Her mind was spinning back to a night during the summer. The night of Austin's birthday, when he'd made dinner for her in his apartment. She'd overheard his brother's message on the answering machine. "The news hits hard, I know," Dave's voice had said. "It gets easier after a while, really it does."

As she looked into Harris's eyes, Sumer knew. How could she not have known?

She went to Harris's side. He took her hand. His own was trembling. They stared out the window at the black, cold night.

"That's okay, Harris," Summer whispered. "You don't have to say it out loud."

"You still awake?" Diana asked Sarah. "It's almost midnight." She knelt beside Sarah's cot, which they'd set up in an empty stall.

"It smells funny in here," Sarah said.

"That's horse. And hay. I kind of like it."

Sarah rubbed her eyes. "Santa won't come to a barn, Diana."

"Vera said he would."

"I miss my mom."

"I know."

"Do you miss your mom?" Sarah asked.

"A little bit."

"Do you miss Seth?"

"Yeah," Diana said. "I miss Seth."

"He'll see you on Christmas, though. He said."

"That's what he said, all right."

"What if my mom doesn't come back? Ever?"

Diana squeezed Sarah's hand. Maybe it was time to stop telling fairy stories about Santa. After Christmas came and went, it'd be time to call social services and send Sarah on her way. Diana's little rescue attempt would be over, and Sarah's nightmare would just be starting.

Diana tried to imagine dropping her off at some cramped, crowded little office in a few days. But she couldn't seem to get her mind around the notion of saying good-bye that way.

"Sometimes, Sarah, people let us down," Diana said. "They don't mean to, maybe. But they do."

"What people?"

Boyfriends. Mothers. Diana sighed. "All kinds of people. Maybe even Santa. Maybe even your mom."

Sarah just stared at her, uncomprehending. Lost. Well, who could blame her, really? Diana thought with sudden anger.

"I have an idea," she said. "Let's open a present."

"It's not Christmas."

"It's almost midnight. That's good enough."

"You open one too."

"Okay. If you say so."

Diana returned to the front of the barn, where her friends were playing poker. She grabbed Mallory's present and the stuffed lamb Summer had wrapped.

When she returned to Sarah's cot, the little girl was sitting up expectantly. "Here," Diana said. "This is from me to you."

Carefully, Sarah unwrapped the gift. It wasn't the frantic clawing Diana remembered from her own childhood. Sarah unwrapped as if the paper itself were a gift.

At last she opened the box. "It's a lamb," she said without much feeling.

"A new lamb. Nice and clean, with no stuffing problems. Isn't he cute?"

Sarah nodded.

"He's bigger too. And he has a little bell around his neck. We could give him a name if you want."

"I already have a lamb." Sarah clutched her old lamb tightly.

"I know. I just thought . . ." Why hadn't she listened to Marquez? Of course Sarah wouldn't want a replacement. It was the only thing from her old life she had to hang onto. "Never mind. Maybe they can be friends."

"You open yours."

Diana stared at her mother's scrawled handwriting on the package. "Why don't we wait until tomorrow? I'm kind of tired."

"You said."

"Okay. But if it's hideous, don't laugh. My mother has eccentric taste."

Diana opened the outer box. Inside was another battered cardboard box. Odd. Mallory usually had things gift-wrapped.

"What is it?" Sarah asked.

"I don't know. Clothes, maybe? Here." Diana passed the box to Sarah. "You open it."

After a couple of tries, Sarah managed to loosen the top of the box, revealing layers of white tissue paper. Diana reached for the small white envelope tucked inside.

"Go ahead," she said without interest. "See what it is."

While Diana opened the envelope, Sarah dug through the tissue paper. Suddenly she gasped.

Diana looked up. Sarah was holding a doll. An old doll with bent wings and a torn white dress and a long tangle of wiry yellow hair.

"She's beautiful," Sarah whispered.

"She's something, all right," Diana murmured as she opened the card.

> D—
>
> *Want you to know I went to every damn secondhand shop in L.A. before I found her. How's that for motherly devotion?*
>
> *I love you.*
>
> *P.S. Her name's Veronica.*

Diana put the card back in its envelope. She felt a tingle creep up her spine. "You like her?" she asked.

"She's an angel, see?"

"Yeah, well, I suppose that could be debated." Diana smiled as she straightened the doll's droopy wings. "How about if you take care of her for me, Sarah?"

"But she's yours."

"I think she'd rather be with you. But get ready, it's real hard work, being a mom—much harder than it looks. I'll help you name her, though. Tomorrow we'll think of a name together."

Sarah considered. "Are you sure?"

"I'm sure," Diana said. She kissed the top of Sarah's head, grateful for the darkness that hid the tears in her eyes. "I have the card. That's all I really need."

17

Santa Comes Through

Summer awoke in the barn early Christmas morning. She sat up on her elbows in her cot. Everyone was asleep except Austin. His sleeping bag was empty.

She put on her shoes and slipped outside. The air was a surprise—wet, cold, still promising a storm. The sky was heavy with low-slung clouds, muting the dawn light.

Summer clutched at her sweater, shivering. Her breath made little clouds. Winter breath. It made her ache for home.

She headed toward the beach. The sand was dark brown, still wet from the storm, pocked and barren as a moonscape. The ocean barely moved.

She'd walked only a few minutes when she spotted Austin. She knew he'd be there. He was sitting on the sand, half hidden by a tall clump of sea grass. He didn't say anything when she sat beside him.

"Merry Christmas," she said softly.

For the first time Austin glanced at her. He looked as if he hadn't slept. "Yeah," he said. "You too."

"Harris and Vera seemed awfully happy last night, huh?"

Austin nodded. "You were right about them. Chalk one up for incurable romanticism."

"You don't sound very happy about it."

"I am." Austin rubbed his eyes. "Really I am. It's just hard to admit that if you'd listened to me, Harris would be all alone in his town house right now, potting some plant. Instead it's like he's starting his life all over again."

The drone of a small plane met their ears, buzzing insistently in the clouds. Suddenly it broke through, skimming their underside as it swooped west.

"Do you remember that day we met on the plane?" Summer said. "How I was trying to cheer you up with this story about that tarot card lady who read my future on my first trip to Florida?"

"I remember, more or less. I was preoccupied at the time, thinking about how blue your eyes were. Trying to figure out how I was ever going to come up with a way to write about them without resorting to some huge cliché."

"That's sweet. But mostly I think you were upset about going to see your dad in the hospital."

"True. I was giving you the Harlequin romance version."

"Well, I went on and on—I was in full babble mode—about how she told me I'd meet three guys that first summer. One mysterious, one dangerous, and one who'd be the right one. And the funny thing was, she turned out to be right." She hesitated. "You asked me if I was sorry about her telling me what was going to happen. About knowing the future."

"And you said you didn't believe in that sort of thing, so it didn't really matter." Austin gazed out at the gray ocean. "But she *was* right."

"No. She wasn't right, not completely. Diver was the mysterious one. And Adam was the dangerous one. But Seth . . . Seth wasn't the right one."

"Who was, then?"

Summer let the question hand in the icy air. "The thing is, you can't know the future, Austin."

"Oh, yes, you can," he said darkly.

Slowly Summer slipped her hand in his. She moved closer, close enough for their shoulders to touch. She looked out at the ocean with him.

"Things change," she whispered. "They'll find a cure, Austin."

Moments passed, filled with the rustle of the sea grass and the murmur of the waves. Summer waited. She couldn't seem to think, or hope, or even breathe. All she could do was sit there, frozen in the sand, and wait.

Finally Austin stood. His stance was rigid, but his shoulders seemed to tremble. He looked at her with hard angry eyes glinting with tears.

"He told you," Austin said, his voice as bitter as the wind.

"No, not exactly. I figured it out." Her voice was choked. She realized she was crying. "I should have known a long time ago. I should have just . . . sensed it. I should have."

"And why is that?"

"Because I love you." Summer reached out her hand, sobbing. "Austin. Please. Don't you see it doesn't matter to me?"

He pulled his hand away. "Don't you see it does matter to me? Don't you see it's the only thing that matters?"

"Austin"

"Leave me alone, Summer." Austin moved away from her down the beach. His tears were falling freely now, his rigid shoulders slumped. "I just can't do this," he whispered. "It isn't worth it. It hurts too much."

He walked several more steps before he turned around again. "Leave me alone for good."

"Santa didn't come," Sarah said as Diana led her into Vera's parlor that morning.

"Sure he did. Look at all the presents under that tree."

"You bought those," Sarah said accusingly.

"Fresh coffee and orange juice for everyone," Vera announced, carrying a silver tray into the room. "Most of our guests have already checked out, so we'll have the place pretty much to ourselves this morning."

"Nice fire, Harris," Marquez said.

"I haven't had a fire in that fireplace in years!" Vera exclaimed. "The thermometer read thirty-three this morning, can you imagine?"

Summer came into the room. Her hair was windblown, and she looked as though she'd been crying. "Summer!" Marquez said. "Where've you been, girl?"

"I went for a walk on the beach," Summer said softly.

"You okay?" Diana asked.

"Fine."

"Did you happen to run into Austin?" Harris asked.

Summer nodded. "I don't know where he is now, though."

"Well, then, I guess my announcement will have to wait," Harris said with a mischievous grin.

"What announcement?" Marquez asked.

Harris put a finger to his lips. "All in good time, my dear."

"So, are we all more or less here?" Vera asked.

"Except for Austin," Diver said.

And Jennie, Diana added silently, hugging Sarah close.

"Let's start." Marquez rubbed her hands together. "Come on, Sarah. You're the one with all the goodies. Open something."

"Where'd the angel doll come from?" Summer asked.

"Mallory," Diana said, smiling. "Not your usual Mallory gift, hmm?"

"I'm sure there's a story there," Summer said questioningly.

Diana nodded. "A long one."

"Tell Summer your angel doll's name, Sarah," Marquez urged.

"Her name's Diana," Sarah said proudly.

Marquez laughed. "No typecasting there."

Vera glanced out the window and moaned. "Oh, dear. More guests, on Christmas morning? Someone's driving up. You go ahead and start opening, Sarah. I'll be right back."

Diana handed Sarah a flat, square package filled with books. "We'll start with the good-for-you-stuff," Marquez added. "I helped with that."

But Sarah wasn't listening. She was busy rummaging through the pile of gifts.

"What are you looking for, hon?" Diana asked gently.

"I thought maybe Santa might have left a note for me. You know."

Diana looked over at her friends helplessly.

"Maybe he got a little mixed up, Sarah," Summer offered. "His sleigh might have gone off course."

"Yeah. Santa's lousy at directions," Marquez added. "Sometimes he gets real mixed up."

"Sometimes," came a soft voice, "moms do too."

Everyone turned. Sarah looked up. Her eyes went wide. "Mom?"

"Come here, sweet pea."

Sarah galloped into Jennie's arms. Behind her stood Seth, car keys in his hand.

"Santa brought my mom!" Sarah cried to Diana.

Jennie sniffled. "Actually, Seth here brought me."

"I just helped out at the end," Seth told Sarah. "Santa did the hard part."

"What are you doing here?" Diana asked, staring in amazement from him to Jennie and back again.

"I made my grandfather and aunt do presents at the

crack of dawn so I could get over here," Seth explained. He paused to kiss her. "On the way, I stopped at your house to check on the storm damage, see if there was anything I could salvage. When I got there, the note you'd left on the door was gone. I figured it had blown away. But just as I was leaving, I passed this girl on the street, carrying a piece of paper. And I don't know why, but I stopped and asked her if she needed a lift."

"I tried to get back sooner, but my car broke down on me," Jennie said, rocking Sarah in her arms. "I'm . . . so sorry about everything. I just kind of went crazy for a minute. I got laid off from my job, and then we got evicted, and it was all just getting so bad. And when I thought about another Christmas with no toys . . ." She hung her head. "It's no excuse, I know. I don't have any excuse."

"Don't cry, Mom. I got lots of presents," Sarah said happily. "An angel doll and a lamb. And Santa's bringing us a house."

"A what?"

"Um, Santa's still kind of working on that one, Sarah," Diana said. "Remember?"

Jennie gazed around the room, taking in sympathetic faces. "I knew you'd take good care of her," she said shyly. "I knew I was right about you."

"I had fun, Mom. I sleeped with a horse. And I made sand castles."

"And she learned how to accessorize," Diana added.

"And I saw Santa," Sarah continued. "He has pimples and he's kind of grouchy."

Jennie kissed Sarah's cheek. "God, I missed you, baby."

Watching Sarah and Jennie together, Diana felt a strong mix of relief and happiness and melancholy. "What will you do now, Jennie?" Diana asked. "About work and all?"

"Um, I don't know, exactly. I've got a friend who's making some money up in Miami as a maid. I thought maybe I'd head up there, see what I can find."

"You know," Vera said, "if you're looking for a job as a maid, Jennie . . ." She shook her head. "I'm sorry. I shouldn't put you on the spot this way. It's just that I could use an extra pair of hands around here desperately. I can only pay a little over minimum wage, but I could include room and board." She paused. "It's just a thought."

Jennie blinked. "You mean . . . live *here*?"

"I know it's a little isolated, but—"

"You mean here? In this house? Here?"

"Yes. For as long as you want."

Sarah whispered something in Jennie's ear.

"What did she say?"

"She said I should do it because they have cookies and a horse," Jennie reported. "She also said I was wrong about Santa being bogus." She nodded at Vera. "I'd be real honored to take you up on your offer. I can start right this minute if you'd like."

"First things first," Vera said laughing. "Your daughter has a few dozen gifts to unwrap, from the look of things."

Jennie looked over at Diana. "She's a lucky girl," she whispered. "Real lucky."

Diana felt tears coming. Damn. "I'll be right back," she said thickly, making a quick getaway to the bathroom.

She was sitting on the floor clutching a wad of toilet paper a few moments later when someone knocked on the door. "It's me, Seth. Open up."

Diana opened the door a crack. "Go away. I look like an idiot, bawling. She's not my kid. I'm relieved to be rid of her."

"Sarah said for me to give this to you. She made it very clear it's a loaner, however."

He opened the door and passed Diana the angel doll. Carefully Diana adjusted the wings and combed her fingers through the doll's thinning hair.

"What's the deal with the doll?"

"Mallory sent her. A peace offering of sorts." Diana wiped her eyes. "She was supposed to make me forget the bad Christmases, I guess."

Seth stroked her cheek gently. "Did it work?"

"No." Diana managed a laugh. "Well, a little. But don't tell Mallory that. I double my wardrobe every year because of her Christmas guilt. Still, I suppose it did kind of surprise me. You did too, actually. I didn't think you'd come."

"You've got to start trusting me sometime, Diana."

"I know. I'm trying."

Seth kissed her softly. "I told you this Christmas would be different. Now will you admit you were wrong?"

"No." Diana smiled. "But I will admit you were a little more right than I gave you credit for." She took his hand. "Come on."

"Where are we going?"

"I saw some mistletoe back there with your name on it."

18

Just Like Real Life

When it started to snow, Summer was by herself. She'd gone for another walk on the beach early that after-noon. To clear her head, she'd told everybody. To think.

It had started stealthily, a few stray, tentative flakes. Starter snow, the kind the uninitiated might have missed. But Summer was not a novice when it came to snow. She could smell it, she could taste it. And with the arrival of those first few flakes, she could tell they were in for a serious snowfall.

It was strange, watching the fat, twirling flakes come to rest on the sand. Watching them melt into the ocean was stranger still, and more beautiful. The faster they came, the more they softened the hard edges of the world. Everything turned hushed and magical.

She loved the beginning of a snowfall, the anticipation, the impossible stillness. It was always this way. No wind, no sound. Even the waves were stunned into silence.

She didn't hear Austin approaching. He was almost beside her before she sensed him near her.

She hadn't seen him since that morning. He looked calmer now, almost relaxed. A dusting of snowflakes covered his hair.

"You got your wish," he said.

"One, anyway." She held out her hand and watched the snow turn to raindrops in her palm. "Where have you been?"

"Walking. I must have covered the whole key. I went back to the inn just now. Vera was wearing Harris's ring."

"I suppose you disapprove."

"You suppose wrong. I think it's just this side of miraculous."

Summer took a deep breath. She wanted to say something, but there was nothing to say. No way to comfort Austin, no way to reach him. She felt hushed and overwhelmed, like the landscape around her.

"I wanted to tell you about me having the gene,

you know," Austin said. "I came close to it a thousand times."

"Why didn't you, then?"

"I just . . . there wasn't . . ."

"Is it because of Esme?" Summer asked. "Did you tell her?"

Austin made a sound close to a laugh. "Oh, Summer. No. That's not it at all." He shook his head. "The point of Esme is that it was never an issue. No cares, no commitments—that's the way Esme likes it. There is no future to worry about with Esme. And don't you see how much easier it is when you don't care?"

Summer looked at him in silence, unsure of what to say.

"I thought I was protecting you by not telling you, Summer," he went on. "I didn't think it was fair to let you care about someone who was going to end up . . . like my dad." He shrugged. "And I was right. It isn't fair."

"Why should you have the right to decide that for me?" Summer demanded. "Why is it your decision?"

"Because I love you, Summer," Austin said. "That's why."

Summer closed her eyes, looking for the right words. "You know, I learned a lot about myself being on my own this fall, Austin. I learned I can do scary things. I learned I'm strong and independent. I learned

I don't have to lean on anyone else, that I can handle things."

"I knew all that the moment I met you."

Summer started to cry. "Then why can't you trust me to be able to handle this? Why can't you let *me* decide if I want to be with you, even if you do get sick someday, even if you . . ." She swallowed a sob. "Why can't you let me decide?"

He looked at her for a long time. The snow kept coming faster, twirling crazily, an icy fog obscuring everything around them—the beach, the ocean, the sky—until all Summer could seem to see was Austin. Just him. Only him.

"Okay," he finally whispered. "I'll let you decide. You tell me how the story ends."

Summer reached up and took his face in her hands. "I'm glad you asked. I happen to know just how it all turns out."

She kissed him as though it were the first time and the last time, telling him all the things there were no words to say. At last she slowly pulled away, laughing, crying.

"Well?" Austin said.

"It snows, and everybody lives happily ever after." Summer smiled. "Just like real life."

Can't wait for summer?
Check out more beach drama in:

by Katherine Applegate

Six Weeks Till Spring Break, and She Doesn't Have a Thing to Wear

Eight juniors departments, thirty-seven bathing suits, and a half-dozen snarling salesladies into her quest, Summer Smith was ready to admit the obvious: She was a freak of nature.

In the overlit dressing room, four Summers stared back at her from full-length mirrors. They all looked somewhere between very dejected and totally annoyed.

Mounds of shimmering Lycra lay at her feet. Tanks. Thongs. Two-pieces. Suits for long torsos. Suits with inflatable boob enhancers. Suits with little tutulike skirts, like the ones mothers wore at the community pool. And then there were the suits that you would never in a gazillion years let your mother see you wearing, not if you ever wanted to leave the house again.

None of them was right.

Six weeks till the spring break to end all spring breaks, and Summer had nothing to wear to Florida.

Obviously there was only one solution. Nude beaches.

Right.

A clerk knocked on the door. "How are we doing in there?"

"We think maybe we should go to Alaska for spring break," the four Summers replied.

The clerk left with a sigh. Summer sighed, too. She was not a freak of nature. There was nothing wrong with her body. She liked her body just the way it was. Seth liked her body just the way it was. Maybe even a little *too* much.

Seth peered over the top of the door. "Want an unbiased male opinion?"

"Seth! Get out of here! They'll arrest you or something."

"There's no one in the dressing room but you. Besides, I'm going stir-crazy out there. You've got to buy something quick, Summer. I'm starting to sense some chemistry with one of the mannequins." He wiggled his eyebrows suggestively. "By the way, you look extremely excellent. Buy that one. Wear it home."

"It's February. It was sleeting on our way to the mall."

"So wear your mittens, too."

"You're no help. You're just a typical boy. As long as there's a lot of skin involved, you're okay with it."

"And that would be . . . wrong?"

Summer let out a long sigh. "What's the matter with me, Seth? Why can't I get my brain to function?"

"You're stressed out. That's why spring vacation was invented."

"But I'm a senior this year. We're not supposed to be stressed." She brightened. "Soon we'll have five days of complete bliss. It'll be just like last summer. No problems, no hassles. Sun. Sand. Surf."

"How about the fourth *s* word?"

"Sleep?"

"I was thinking about the one that ends in *x*."

Summer batted at him playfully. "I like a guy who's not afraid to dream."

She flipped through a bunch of suits on a hook. "It's between this black tank and that blue two-piece."

"The blue one. Definitely. *Now* can we go? My Egg McMuffin wore off hours ago."

"I need an objective *girl* opinion. I wish Marquez and Diana were here. I ought to call them."

"We'll be seeing them soon enough," Seth said flatly.

"Try to fake a little enthusiasm," Summer chided. "We'll have plenty of time to ourselves over spring break. And Diana's the one who's snagging us the yacht. The rest of the spring breakers will be cramped in mildewy hotel rooms while we'll be living in the lap of luxury."

"I just wish I could have you all to myself," Seth said, gazing at her with a familiar look that was half lust, half love.

She stood on tiptoe, and they kissed over the top of the door. A harsh voice inquired, "And how are we doing in here *now?*"

"We *were* doing great," Seth muttered. He gave the salesclerk a sheepish smile before slinking off. "Buy the two-piece," he called.

The salesclerk shook her head. "I like that black tank, personally. It's very slimming."

Summer groaned. "Do you guys have a pay phone?"

The cell phone was ringing, but that didn't mean they had to pick it up, did it? Maria Marquez felt way too good, with the sun melting into her bones and the ocean lapping at her feet.

Next to her, Diana Olan stirred. "Are you deaf or what?"

"I've got sun-stun. Besides, it's your phone."

"I can't answer it. It might be my mother."

Marquez rolled onto her side. Fine white sand coated her Hawaiian Tropic-ed arm. She grimaced. "All right, chill, I'm coming," she muttered, digging through the canvas beach bag. She sat up, flipped open the phone, and collapsed with the effort. "Yeah?" she asked, adjusting her sunglasses.

"Marquez! Why are you answering Diana's phone? It's me, Summer! I'm at the Mall of America, and I need fashion help!"

"It's your cousin," Marquez reported to Diana. "She's having a mall crisis."

Diana lowered her shades. "Is she with Seth?"

"Is Seth with you?" Marquez asked Summer.

"He's at the food court. Eating fried cheese on a stick."

"Seth's having a fine-dining experience," Marquez said.

Diana nodded, apparently satisfied, and lay back on her towel.

"I haven't talked to you in ages," Marquez chided Summer. "What's up?"

"My parents got the last phone bill and freaked. Between you and Diana and Seth, I'm going to have to get a full-time job to pay for the long distance. I'm using up the last of my quarters on this call."

"Soon it won't be long distance," Marquez

reminded her. "Guess where we are! This will get you psyched. We are lazing by the beach and it's eighty-one degrees and we've got my iPod speakers cranked up and there are four guys playing volleyball not fifty feet from here and they have *definitely* been hitting the gym."

"It's thirty degrees here and sleeting. Why are you looking at other guys? Is everything okay with J.T.?"

"I guess." Marquez adjusted her bathing suit strap. "He's just a little, I don't know, distracted. Anyway, a girl can look, can't she?"

"Ask her how she and Seth are doing," Diana prompted.

Marquez shot her a dirty look. "I answered the phone, I ask the questions." She rolled onto her side. "So how are you and Sethie doing? Still drooling?"

"It's hard to do much drooling when he's in Wisconsin and I'm in Minnesota. He has to drive back this afternoon."

"Well, soon you two will have your own little love nest, courtesy of cousin Di. I saw a picture of the yacht," Marquez said. "I mean, this is some spring break hangout, Summer. Chandeliers and water beds and a big-screen TV. Oh, yeah, and a Jacuzzi in the shape of a heart, can you believe it?"

"This is going to be such a cool vacation." Summer sighed. "I miss you guys so much. I know I just saw you both at Christmas, but it seems like forever."

"We miss you, too. It's just way too weird, me and Diana hanging out together solo. We need you around to keep us from trying to kill each other."

"I know what you mean," Summer said. Her voice was distant. "Diver and I have been going at it, too."

"Your sweet, innocent, incredibly gorgeous brother?" Marquez demanded. "I can't imagine Diver having a negative emotion. He's like . . . all Zen about everything."

"Not lately. Not like last summer." Summer sighed again. "I wish we were all back together. I wish everything was the way it was last summer, you know?"

"Yeah, I do. And it will be soon. Just a month or so."

"Six weeks, four days, and a few hours. But it's not like I'm obsessed or anything."

Marquez laughed. "So what's the fashion emergency?"

"Oh. I almost forgot. It's down to two choices. Two-piece, barely there, electric blue. Or black tank, fits really well, would be really good for swimming and jet-skiing and stuff."

"Summer, Summer, Summer. This is spring break, girl. In Florida, not Minne-so-dead. Definitely the two-piece."

"I can't wait to see you," Summer said softly.

"I have to hang up now before the quarters run out, okay?"

"I'll call you next time."

"You're broke, too."

Marquez smirked at Diana. "Yeah, but Diana isn't."

Diana sat up and grabbed the phone. "Summer? I just wanted to say . . ." She turned away from Marquez, lowering her voice. "I just wanted to say I really miss you. . . . Yeah. Me too. . . . Yeah. Buy the two-piece, okay?"

She tossed the phone into her beach bag. Marquez stared at her, incredulous.

"What?" Diana demanded.

"'I really miss you'?" Marquez parroted. "Have you been out in the sun too long? If I didn't know you better, I'd swear that was like, you know, an actual emotion."

Diana almost looked hurt. "I like Summer a lot. I was a little hard on her last summer, but once I got to know her. . . . Anyway, she *is* my cousin."

Marquez eyed Diana suspiciously. "Still, you're being awfully nice to us, setting up this yacht and all. This isn't even your spring break. You graduated last year, remember?"

"But I kind of missed mine. So I'm compensating."

"You're compensating for *something*," Marquez said

with a grin. "But I just can't figure out what."

"Oh, Maria," Diana said, knowing how much Marquez hated being called by her first name. "Such a suspicious little mind. With the emphasis on *little*."

Marquez closed her eyes. The sun was like a sleeping potion. She'd figure out Diana another day, when she wasn't in a solar coma.

Next to her, Diana sighed. "She'll buy the tank, you know."

Marquez smiled fondly. "I know."

Good-byes Without Yawns and Good-byes Without Explanation

"I miss you already," Seth whispered.

They were parked in his dilapidated Ford in front of Summer's home. He pulled her close—not an easy task, since they both had on down jackets—and lowered his lips to hers. It was a familiar kiss, warm and soft, and it occurred to her how comfortable she was with his safe, reliable, always-just-the-same kisses. How many times had he kissed her like this? Hundreds? Maybe even thousands?

To her horror, Summer suddenly felt a yawn coming. She tried to stifle it, forcing her mouth to stay closed, but it was no use. She yawned hugely. Her mouth opened to cavelike proportions.

Seth pulled away. "Sorry," he snapped. "Was I boring you?"

"You could never bore me," Summer said, placing her hand over his. "I'm just . . . I'm really sorry."

He ran his fingers through his thick chestnut hair. It was shorter than he'd worn it the previous summer, when they'd met, and his tan had faded to Wisconsin pale. But the great brown eyes hadn't changed—laughing and intense and thoughtful at the same time.

"*I* thought we were having a passionate kiss."

"We were. I didn't sleep very well last night, is all. My parents were fighting with Diver again." She made a little circle on the steamed-up window.

"So I wasn't putting you to sleep?"

"No! Was I putting *you* to sleep?"

"You're the one who yawned." After a moment Seth managed a lopsided grin. He patted her thigh. "Sorry. It'll be okay with Diver. He's just having a hard time right now."

"I guess."

Seth checked the stick-on clock on the peeling dashboard and sighed. "I need to get going."

"I feel like all we do is say good-bye to each other." Summer reached into the backseat to retrieve her shopping bags. "Wait, I almost forgot!" she exclaimed. "I bought you some stuff for the trip."

"So that's what took you so long. Cool. Presents!"

They weren't just presents, they were part of a scientifically designed plan to rekindle her romance with Seth. Summer knew about rekindling because she read her mother's *New Woman* magazine sometimes, and revving up a romance seemed to be a big concern for couples like her parents, not that she wanted to think about *that* too much. And since she and Seth were a long-term couple of nearly nine months (Summer insisted on counting from the day they'd met), she figured it might be time for a little rekindling.

Toward that end, she'd bought some of the items suggested in the article. Candles. A book called *101 Love Poems to Set the Mood*. A bottle of coconut-almond-papaya-scented suntan oil for rubbing on Seth's back while they basked in the Florida sun. And, from one of those Spencer kind of stores, a watch without hands. It was meant to symbolize that they weren't going to think about anything but each other. Seth was kind of obsessive about time.

Slowly Seth examined the items, one by one. He lingered on the tanning oil, grinning. When he got to the watch, he groaned.

"It's symbolic," Summer explained. "Five days without time pressures."

"You know, it's not like I'm obsessed," Seth said irritably. "Just because I know that when the big hand's on the twelve and the little hand's on the three it means it's three o'clock."

"I already said I was sorry at the mall," Summer snapped. "I lost track of time." They were doing it again. They always had nitpicky little fights right before saying good-bye.

Seth stroked her hair apologetically. "Thanks for all the cool stuff. Will you pack it for me? I'm just taking my backpack." He made a big ceremony of putting on the watch. Then he passed her a small paper sack from the backseat. "Here. For you, for the big trip. I went shopping, too."

She opened the bag. "Zinc oxide!" she said. It was precisely the same voice she used every Christmas when she opened one of her great-aunt's handmade sweaters.

"Green. For your nose, 'cause you know how you burn."

Summer smiled. "Thanks." It occurred to her that rekindling their romance might be more work than she'd thought.

She kissed Seth good-bye. In her mind, she was not in an uninspectable 1982 Ford with a hole in the floorboard. She was not wearing two pairs of thick wool socks in her Doc Martens. In her mind, she was already in Florida, touched by hibiscus-scented tropical breezes. The ocean was churning gently, waves breaking on a pristine white beach. The sun was kissing her bare shoulders with soothing heat.

This kiss, she didn't yawn once.

"Bought you something."

Summer tossed her Dayton's bag. As usual, her brother was lying on the couch in the family room. *Oprah* was on. Diver's blue eyes were slitted like a dozing cat's.

"It's a book," Summer said. She plopped down onto the La-Z-Boy, her legs draped over the arm. *"Guide to Southeastern Coastal Birds."*

Diver brushed his blond hair out of his eyes. It was darker than it had been the summer before. The gold streaks from sun and salt water were gone, and he'd cut it at their parents' insistence. He studied the cover, which featured a prehistoric-looking pelican. "Cool," he said vaguely. "Thanks."

"It's for when we go down for spring break. Aren't you getting excited about it? Going back to Florida, I mean? It's been six months since we've seen a palm tree, Diver. Or the ocean. Or a big, fat, sunburned, hairy-backed tourist in a Speedo."

Diver smiled wistfully. "Or a pelican. I miss Frank."

"Me, too," Summer said, recalling the mega-pooping pelican who'd resided on their porch.

"Sometimes it all seems so unreal," Diver said. He looked at Summer with the clear, innocent gaze that often made her feel as though he were the younger sibling, even though he was two years older. "Last summer, I mean, and finding you, and then coming here, and Jack and Kim, and . . . you know."

It still bothered Summer when he said that. Jack and Kim. Jack and Kim were Mom and Dad, his mom and dad, and hers. She didn't understand why Diver couldn't call them that, after all they'd suffered through. Why he couldn't say two little words.

Of course, her parents were no better. They called him Jonathan, when he was clearly Diver and always would be.

Summer grabbed the remote and switched to CNN. Diver didn't even blink. "I talked to Diana and Marquez today. Aunt Mallory has this friend with a yacht we can use."

Diver nodded noncommittally. He was thumbing through the bird book.

"Diver," Summer asked suddenly, "do you wish you'd stayed in Crab Claw Key? Do you hate it here in Minnesota?"

He smiled. It was pure smile, the kind of smile that she'd watched melt a hundred female hearts at Bloomington High School. "Well, it's very cold here," he said, as if that were an answer.

Their mother appeared in the doorway. Her coat was damp. She grimaced at Diver. "I thought you were working today."

"I called in sick." Lately Diver had been working as a stock boy at Target.

"Jonathan, this is just what happened with Burger King—"

Summer winced. She did not want to be around for this. "Mom, I got a great bathing suit," she interrupted. "Two, actually. Will you tell me what you think?"

Her mother hesitated, eyes flickering between Summer and Diver. "I've got a ton of groceries in the trunk," she said. "Come help." She pointed a finger at Diver. "We'll talk later."

Diver did not answer. He was tracing the pelican photo with his finger. "Frank had more brown here, around the eyes."

"I'll get the groceries," Summer said to her mother. "You check out my bathing suits. They're in the Dayton's bag. And try not to react like a mom, okay?"

Her mother gazed at Diver. "That's harder than you think," she said softly.

Summer lay in bed, her quilt tucked up around her chin. It was quiet. Finally.

There'd been another fight that evening. Slammed doors, loud voices. Mostly her parents' voices. Diver hardly ever argued. He just absorbed other people's words.

Sometimes she still had the dream. The one about the little boy chasing a red ball, about the day Diver had been lost to the family. Summer hadn't even been born yet, of course, so the dream was just a collage of stories from her parents, from news clippings, and from Diver's own vague recollections. Not that he remembered much. He'd been kidnapped, he'd grown up knowing two other parents as his own, they'd been abusive, he'd run away.

Maybe he'd been on his own too long. Maybe that was why, when he and Summer had found each other by some crazy miracle the summer before, he hadn't seemed entirely sure about coming back to the family that was really his own. He was uncomfortable with rules and curfews and schoolwork. He didn't quite belong in Minnesota.

Summer slept fitfully. She kept hearing things: her door, a creak in the hallway, a sound from downstairs. She dreamed she was lying on a couch by the edge of the ocean, watching a pelican toss a little red ball in the air, then catch it in his great beak. Diver was there, too, but he was watching her. He said something, two words she could not quite make out, and then he dove into the water, swimming slowly away until he was just a speck on the horizon.

She woke up shivering beneath her quilt. Her pillow was wet with tears. It was a bleak, gray dawn. She sat up a little, quilt pulled close, and then she noticed the torn sheet of notebook paper on the edge of her bed.

She saw Diver's scrawl and the two words she had not been able to hear in her dream: *I'm sorry.*

And she knew he was really gone.

About the Author

After Katherine Applegate graduated from college, she spent time waiting tables, typing (badly), watering plants, wandering randomly from one place to the next with her boyfriend, and just generally wasting her time. When she grew sufficiently tired of performing brain-dead minimum-wage work, she decided it was time to become a famous writer. Anyway, a writer. Writing proved to be an ideal career choice, as it involved neither physical exertion nor uncomfortable clothing, and required no social skills.

Ms. Applegate has written more than one hundred books under her own name and a variety of pseudonyms. She has no children, is active in no organizations, and has never been invited to address a joint session of Congress. She does, however, have an evil, foot-biting cat named Dick, and she still enjoys wandering randomly from one place to the next with her boyfriend.

Pulse It

Did you love this book?

Want to get access to the hottest books for free?

Log on to simonandschuster.com/pulseit

to find out how to join,

get access to cool sweepstakes,

and hear about your favorite authors!

Become part of Pulse IT and tell us what you think!

 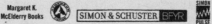